"Running out on me again, are you?"

"It's better this way," Linzi whispered.

"Why?"

"You brought me here — so that you could torment me," she flung back. "Don't you understand? We were getting married for the wrong reasons, not because we *loved* each other — as adults should love."

"Well, we're *both* grown up now." He ran one hand with exquisite tenderness down the length of her body.

If she let Jason possess her now, there would be no leaving. And the hurt her staying would cause him would be worse than any simple rejection. She couldn't let it happen.

"It's no use," she said wearily, letting her eyes run over his body. "You're just not persuasive enough. Now — let me go."

Jason's face contorted with fury. "After that, I'll only be too pleased."

Carver's Bride

Nicola West

Harlequin Books

TORONTO • NEW YORK • LONDON
AMSTERDAM • PARIS • SYDNEY • HAMBURG
STOCKHOLM • ATHENS • TOKYO • MILAN

Original hardcover edition published in 1982
by Mills & Boon Limited

ISBN 0-373-02646-3

Harlequin Romance first edition September 1984

Printed in U.S.A.

CHAPTER ONE

'JUST who *is* that artist you're going to sit for?' Richard Fabian asked, his smooth, rather plump face creased with suspicion. 'Do you really mean to say you don't know?'

Linzi Berwick looked at him and sighed. She had to admit, it did seem strange—that she should be asked for specially for a modelling job by an artist who refused to give his name. Particularly as, except for a few small assignments, she wasn't really an artist's model anyway. But Anna, her agent, had insisted that it was a condition of the contract. For publicity reasons, she had implied—the artist had apparently had problems with newspaper reporters at his previous home and now he had found this remote hideaway he didn't intend that anyone should disturb him there. It sounded reasonable enough to Linzi, who had cause herself to be cautious where newspapers were concerned, but she didn't know if she could explain it to Richard.

'He's doing a special piece of work, too,' she told him, remembering all she could of the few facts her agent had been able to give her. 'That's what he wants me for. Something quite big, apparently.'

'What sort of thing?' Richard still wasn't satisfied. 'A picture? I hope there's going to be nothing—er—distasteful about it,' he added, his voice disapproving.

Linzi felt herself flush at the implication and turned away quickly. If only Richard knew! But she'd never told him the real reason why she'd returned from a successful modelling career in New York. That was something she intended to keep strictly to herself.

'You ought to know me better than that,' she said in a

low voice. She crossed to the mirror and stood staring into it, lifting her mane of chestnut hair to reveal the long, slim neck that had earned her the nickname of 'Swan'. She scarcely noticed the slender figure, a little above average height, or the glowing topaz eyes that matched the golden-brown hair. To her, they were just the tools of her trade, to be cared for but taken very much for granted. But she did notice the shadows that lurked in the tawny depths of the eyes that had looked out from so many magazine covers; and she saw too the beginnings of a tiny line of worry between her finely-shaped brows.

Worry? When she had so much to look forward to? When she was about to become the wife of a successful banker, to enter society at his side and to leave behind her the uncertain world of modelling, the long struggle that had brought her to a peak of success that could, nevertheless, at any moment be toppled? Linzi shrugged her shoulders impatiently and turned away to face Richard again. Worry must have become a habit in these past few months. Now it could be forgotten. In a matter of weeks she would be preparing for her wedding.

But before that, there was this last mysterious job, the one which was causing Richard such concern. And for some reason Linzi wanted very badly to do it. In a dim way she knew that it could be a fitting end to her modelling career, something that would mean more to her in future years than any of the glossy magazine pictures or TV videos she had so carefully stored away. Something that would give her the comfort of knowing that all the struggle had been worthwhile.

She crossed the room to Richard's side and knelt beside his chair, touching his hair with her fingers. She knew that Richard, so conventional and orderly, was disturbed by the bizarre way in which she had been engaged to do the job, and she understood that to his orthodox mind there could only be something suspicious in such a secretive method of finding an artist's model. But to Linzi, the whole affair was exciting and intriguing. She felt she could not bear to refuse and never know who the artist was, or what he wanted her to sit for. And when, gazing at Richard's still furrowed brow and wary eyes, she wondered if perhaps she ought, after all, to refuse, she told herself quickly that they weren't married yet; that Richard was, anyway, setting off tomorrow on a tour of Europe for his bank; and that by the time he returned she too would be back in London, ready to prepare for their marriage.

'Don't worry, darling,' she said softly. 'I'm sure there's nothing sinister in it. Anna told me he's a very well-known artist, but until I've agreed definitely to take the job he doesn't want her to say who he is. That's understandable, isn't it—if he doesn't want any publicity. I might say no and then go and tell some reporter and blow the whole thing! And I promise that if there *is* anything I don't like, I'll come straight back to London, contract or no contract!'

'It's not as if I even knew where you were going,' Richard grumbled. 'It could be anywhere. The wilds of Scotland—Ireland—Northumbria——'

'Or Hereford or Hampshire,' Linzi teased him. 'Richard, don't you trust me? I'm still the girl you proposed to, you know. I haven't changed in the past five weeks. And you liked me enough then.'

'Of course I trust you!' he replied quickly—a little too quickly? Linzi wondered. 'It isn't that. It's just—well, the whole thing's rather silly, if you ask me. All this secrecy. Anna should have been able to tell you the real situation, so that you could make a proper assessment. And then I could have gone away tomorrow knowing just where you were, who you were with and what you were doing. As it is . . .'

His words trailed away into a dissatisfied silence and Linzi felt a quirk of disquiet. Was he always going to insist on knowing her every movement after they were married? But she shook the thought away. It was simply the natural concern of a newly-engaged man. Richard's own life, surely, was far too busy for him to be worrying every moment about his wife's activities. Not that there'd be anything for him to worry about; Linzi was too grateful for his love and attentions to want to do anything that would upset him.

Richard had come into Linzi's life at a crucial moment. Newly returned from New York, where she had spent the last eighteen months, she had been unsure of what to do next. Modelling was the only thing she knew—she had been working her way to the top for the past five years—but she felt that it had gone sour on her. Luckily, she had saved enough money not to have to work immediately, but she also knew that living in London was now astronomically expensive and that she would have to make a decision before too long. In any case, she must go to see her agent. Anna had befriended Linzi when she had first arrived in London, lost and unhappy, at the age of eighteen. She had guided her through the first uncertain steps in her career, seeing in her a promise Linzi had never recognised in herself, seeing that the lanky, ungainly figure could be turned into something graceful and sensuous, that the wild mop of russet hair could be coaxed into a beautiful and manageable mane.

So it had been Anna to whom Linzi first went on her return from America. Anna, hectically busy as ever, who fell on her with a cry of delight and swept her off at once for lunch at a quiet restaurant where they could talk uninterrupted.

'Give up modelling!' Anna had cried when they had dispensed with all the news of mutual friends and enemies and were discussing themselves again. 'Linzi, you have to be joking. Why, you're at the top of the tree now. The editors and photographers will be clamouring for you. I can think of half a dozen jobs I could get for you right now. You *can't* give up!'

Linzi's glowing eyes were unusually sombre as she gazed at her old friend. Anna had known all about her from the moment they first met—but now there was something that even she was not to be told. Oh, she would have understood, she would probably have tried to jolly Linzi out of her feelings and told her she was worrying over nothing, that every successful model had to take the rough with the smooth—but what had happened had hurt Linzi too deeply to be talked over, even with such an understanding friend. It had to remain secret. And that being so, she could not easily explain her decision to give up modelling. She could only shrug and mutter something about needing a change.

'Well, we all need a holiday now and then,' Anna told her. 'I'm crying out for one myself. Look—why don't we go together, at the end of the summer, perhaps? Really get away from it all. Or maybe there's some other reason why you want to give up the modelling scene?' Her eyes sharpened as she looked with fresh interest at the younger girl. 'Don't say you've found a man at last—that paragon you've been looking for all these years!'

To her annoyance, Linzi felt a warm blush travelling up her neck and over her face to the roots of her hair. 'No, of course not,' she said sharply, and then wished she hadn't been so vehement. Anna might just have accepted that as an excuse. 'You know I'm not interested in men.'

'Do I?' Anna regarded her thoughtfully. 'Well, maybe I do. Men in general, that is. But are you sure you're not still carrying a torch for one in particular? One—*Jason*—wasn't that his name?'

Linzi bit her lip. She wanted to snap at Anna, tell her to mind her own business, that Jason was buried deeply in her past and she didn't want to discuss him anyway. But just in time she realised that such a sharp retort would only intensify Anna's suspicion that she still harboured a feeling for him. And that, after all these years, was something she wouldn't—couldn't—tolerate. Ever since her first arrival in London her whole life and career had been geared to forgetting Jason Carver. Surely, by now, she was entitled to believe that she had.

There was only one way to remove that interested look from Anna's face. And after all, would it be so bad? She knew the London modelling scene. She hadn't been away long enough to be forgotten, and in any case her success in America must stand her in good stead now she was back. And she had to earn some money somehow—and this was the best, the only way she knew.

'All right,' she said, picking up her wineglass and tossing back its contents as if to seal a pledge, 'I'll come back to modelling. I suppose I meant to all along. Perhaps I just wanted to try my wings a little.'

'Your wings don't need any trying,' Anna said fondly. 'You could do anything you put your mind to, Linzi, and you know it. But it's a shame to waste that perfect figure and gorgeous hair, and those amazing eyes, just sitting at a desk typing, or whatever it is you thought you might do instead. You're in your prime now, Linzi, and you're going to stay there for quite a while.' She picked up her own glass and held it against Linzi's. 'To the future, my dear. May you have everything you desire.'

And it seemed that her good wishes were to come true. Linzi had, once she had made up her mind, thrown herself into her resumption of her career with all her usual enthusiasm and was soon working hard. Editors liked her because she drew the customers—people were more likely to buy an issue of their magazine if it featured Linzi Berwick. Photographers liked her because Linzi respected their work and co-operated with them, never complaining at the long hours spent in unsuitable clothes—furs in August, swimsuits in January—and because she was photogenic enough to reward their efforts with interest. Manufacturers liked her because she could make anything look good. And the women who bought fashion magazines—and the men, too, who glanced surreptitiously at those left lying about by their wives and girl-friends—took her to their hearts.

Linzi had been in London for a little under two months when she met Richard.

Kneeling beside him now, stroking his thinning hair with gentle fingers, she remembered the party. She had been invited, along with the photographer and other members of the publicity team, to celebrate the launching of a new business enterprise just outside London. Linzi had never fully understood what the new enterprise was producing—high finance had always been rather beyond her—but she had enjoyed the party, held at the home of the chairman of the board, and it was as she stood on the spacious lawns, sipping champagne, that she had first caught Richard's eye and found him approaching her purposefully across the grass.

'You must feel at a distinct disadvantage here,' he had told her, smiling. 'Everyone knows your name and face so well! I'm Richard Fabian. You won't have heard of me— I'm a banker.'

'A behind-the-scenes man,' Linzi suggested, and he nodded.

'Exactly.' His light blue eyes regarded her seriously. 'I was wondering what arrangements you have for getting back to town. I've got my car here—thought we might have dinner on the way back.'

Linzi was half amused, half intrigued. Richard Fabian, impeccably if unadventurously dressed, didn't strike her as the type to pick up girls at parties. But he looked a pleasant enough man; just the solid, reliable sort of person you'd expect to be a banker. And, feeling suddenly that it would be a pleasant change to get away, for once, from the rather hectic company of the publicity team, she nodded. 'I'd like that.'

That dinner had been the first of many. Linzi had found in Richard an undemanding companion, one who would listen courteously to her stories of modelling life, her joys and her woes, yet remain firmly but quietly apart from it all. In his company she found herself able to relax and rest in a way that was impossible with her other friends. There was even a kind of repose in listening to him talk about his own work, although Linzi found most of what he said almost impossible to follow.

Before long she was seeing Richard several times a week. And when he had to go away for a fortnight, on banking business abroad, she was surprised to find herself missing him more than she had expected. On his return, she could see that he too had found her absence from his side leaving a bigger gap than anticipated. And when, after a particularly good dinner in a romantic, candlelit restaurant, he asked her to marry him, Linzi knew that she had been expecting his proposal.

'Marry?' she said doubtfully. 'Are you sure, Richard? Sure that I'd be suitable?'

'Quite sure,' he replied, and laid his hand over hers. 'I've thought it over very carefully, Linzi. It's time I married. I need a wife—oh, to run my home, to help me with my entertaining, all sorts of things. And—well, I'd like a family, too. Every since I met you, my dear, I've felt that perhaps you would be the one I could ask to share my life, be a mother to my children. I feel that more and more strongly. And I've hoped, lately, that perhaps you may feel it too.' He looked at her, his eyes anxious and appealing.

'My job——' she began slowly, and Richard interrupted eagerly.

'You need never work another day. I can support us both in ample comfort, I promise you that. Oh, I know you've enjoyed it—and you've made a success of it, too. But somehow I feel you're ready to give it up for something better. Marriage and all that it means. Comfort, security, your own home and family—isn't that what every woman wants, even in these days of liberation?'

Linzi felt a stab of irritation at his casual dismissal of the career she'd worked so hard at. But she followed it quickly with a reminder that it must, after all, seem very small beer to Richard with his constant dealings in international finance. She looked thoughtfully at his good-natured face, creased a little now with anxiety as he waited for her reply. He would be a good, reliable husband, never asking more than she could give. With him, she could look forward to a life of comparative luxury—perhaps a house somewhere in the country—and, as he had suggested, total security. It was that that attracted her most. The thought of the security she had missed so much since her teens; the security that had once surrounded her life, only to be cruelly torn away, not once but twice. . . .

Linzi bit her lip as an unwanted image of a tall, craggy-faced man with black hair and searingly blue eyes swam into her mind. With an almost perceptible effort she pushed him back down into the layers of her subconscious where he belonged. That was *years* ago, she admonished herself, even more strictly than she had Anna. It was in the past. Dead. Buried.

So why was she still letting it affect her? Why was she still letting the memory of that painful time prevent her from enjoying what Richard had so correctly guessed she longed for—marriage to a kind husband, a happy and secure home, children of her own? Was it because she had once cherished a hope that those children might, too, have wild black hair and brilliant blue eyes?

She looked up and met Richard's eyes across the table. Brown hair instead of black; pale blue eyes instead of deep navy. But a kindness and steadiness that she thought she needed. With him there would be no storms, no wild passion. But there would, instead, be havens; peaceful harbours. And maybe that, after all, was the better choice.

Thinking of this now, Linzi was tempted once again to tell Richard she would turn down the mysterious job. But again that tiny imp of rebellion stirred within her. Why *should* she give up a job that tantalised and attracted her so much? She was still her own person, entitled to make her own decisions. And if she did turn it down, what would she do with herself alone in London while he was away, with no work? No, it would be better to go, to satisfy her curiosity, to take on this one last assignment that even now she felt must be in some way important to her.

'Leave me a list of telephone numbers where I can reach you,' she said. 'Or ring through to Anna and let her know. I'll keep in touch, Richard, I promise, and of course if there *is* any funny business, I'll be back so fast London won't know I've gone. But I'm sure there won't be. Honestly, you don't have anything to worry about.' She laughed. 'Why, you'll be in worse peril in all those foreign countries than I shall be! Just watch where you go and don't let any beautiful spies worm the bank's secrets out of you!'

'Of course I shan't! What an idea!' Richard looked shocked, and Linzi sighed a little. His inability to see her jokes worried her a little. But only a little, she told herself firmly. It wasn't really important, and he was beginning, gradually, to understand when she wasn't being serious. And he was so kind and so obviously fond of her that she found it difficult to criticise something he really couldn't help.

'I'll really have to be going now,' he added, glancing at his watch. 'I've an early start in the morning.' He stood up and Linzi stood too, laying her hands lightly on his shoulders. 'Goodnight, my dear. I hope everything goes well—and you *will* be careful, won't you? Insist that this—this artist lets you use his phone, and give me his number so that I can ring you. He can't object to that, since we're engaged. And don't stay a moment longer than you have to.'

'I won't.' She waited for his kiss and felt his lips touch her forehead, his usual way of saying goodnight. Suddenly she wanted more and lifted her face to his, linking her hands behind his neck to draw him closer. Richard's lips were warm and moist against hers and for a moment she almost recoiled. Then she pressed closer to him. This was the man she was going to *marry*! She felt his arms holding her and gave a tiny sigh of relief. He did want her, she knew that—but his principles and respect for her—old-fashioned, some might have said—combined with her own dislike of casual touching and kissing, had kept them farther apart than most engaged couples. She would put that right as soon as he returned from his tour, she promised herself silently. It was ridiculous to allow the standards she had imposed on herself during the past five years to interfere with her relationship with the man she was going to marry. Habit might die hard—but die it must. And as an extra confirmation of that, she nuzzled Richard's cheek for a moment before letting him go.

'It won't be long,' she said softly. 'And then we'll be busy planning the wedding, and looking for somewhere to live. I promise I shan't be taking on any more strange assignments in faraway places.'

She wished then she hadn't said that, for the suspicion returned to Richard's eyes and for a moment he looked as if he might be going to start the argument again. But the chiming of the mantelpiece clock distracted his attention; he glanced at it and gave an exclamation.

'I really must go!' His kiss this time was swift. 'Look after yourself, Linzi—I'll see you when I get back. I've contacted a few estate agents and we should have quite a list to work through then. Goodbye!'

He picked up the briefcase he had left in the tiny hall and was gone, hurrying towards the lift as if it were about to be switched off. Linzi watched him disappear, then went back into her flat and closed the door. She was disturbed by an odd feeling that there was something missing. Well, of course there was, she scolded herself. Richard had gone, hadn't he—and she wouldn't be seeing him again for several weeks. But it was more than that—something to do with the relationship between Richard and herself.

Once more the image of a tall, muscular man, black-haired and with a face like a cliff, whose crags could settle into a frown of thunderous darkness, or light up with a smile of devastating charm, floated across her mind. She stifled an impatient exclamation at the persistence of a memory that should have faded and died years ago, and went into the kitchen to make herself a hot drink. But this time she couldn't push the picture from her mind. It stayed there, taunting and tantalising, until at last she went into her bedroom and fished out an old photograph album, sitting on the bed to look at it while her drink grew cold and unappetising.

The photographs were, to anyone else, just ordinary snapshots. To Linzi, they were all she had left of a way of life that she had lost. As she gazed at them, tears blurred her sight, yet she saw them as clearly in her mind as though their subjects were there with her—or she with them. Picnics on the Sussex Downs with her parents; swimming parties at the coast or on family holidays. Camping scenes, with firelight flickering on the walls of a tent and the murmuring of her parents' voices as she lay drifting off to sleep. Snow and ice on the winter holiday they'd taken one Christmas and she'd learned to ski and fallen for the charming ski instructor. Other Christmases at home, with fun and laughter as her father carved the turkey and her mother produced a pudding wreathed in flames.

And in every picture, that other face. Strong, individual, forceful, yet never overbearing. The face of a man who could dominate, who would always have his own way, yet who had never failed to defer to either her mother or her father, who had never forgotten the deep respect he felt for them or the debt he owed them.

Jason Carver. The man whose black hair and blue eyes Linzi had hoped to see in her own children. The man who had caused her to run away to London at the age of eighteen, to make her own way in the world, to sink or swim on her own account. The man whose effect on her had been so powerful that she had sworn never to marry, never to allow any other man to dominate both her life and emotions in that way again.

The man she had jilted, only a week before their wedding date, five long years ago.

It was late afternoon when Linzi drove her scarlet Mini into the small Welsh town of Crickhowell a few days after Richard had left for his European tour. Doubtfully, she pulled up in the square and took out her map, along with the instructions given her by Anna. There was still an air of mystery about them; even now she had not been told the name of the artist she was to sit for. But at present that was the least of Linzi's worries. Tired by the long drive, a little nervous of the wild hills she had been passing through, she wanted only to find her destination, have some tea and rest.

'Can I help you, miss?' Startled, she looked up into the brown face of an elderly man who was peering into the car. Thankfully, Linzi wound her window right down and showed him Anna's sketch map.

'I'm looking for a house called Bron Melyn,' she told him. 'I know it's up one of the little roads out of Crickhowell, but I'm not sure which.'

'Bron Melyn, is it?' The bright old eyes looked at her with interest. 'You'll be one of those artist people, then? Eh, the games they have up there sometimes!' He chuckled wheezily and Linzi stared at him, disturbed by his words. *Games*? Were Richard's premonitions to be proved right after all? She opened her mouth, wanting to ask the old man more but uncertain how to phrase it, but before she could speak he was leaning through the window, pointing up a narrow road that led out of one corner of the square.

'Now, you take that road there, see, and follow it up as

far as you can go. Don't take no side turnings and don't worry when it gets a bit rough. They has all sorts going up and down that little old track!' He paused to laugh again. 'All sorts!' he repeated, shaking his head and wiping his eyes. 'Just follow it as far as you can go, you can't miss Bron Melyn.'

Linzi thanked him, and he withdrew to the side of the road and watched with a proprietorial air as she drove out of the square. Her uneasiness returned. Just what had he meant by *games*? And his subsequent remark about 'all sorts' going up the track—that had sounded odd, too. What had he meant—and why had it amused him so much?

Linzi had promised Richard that she would go straight back to London if everything didn't seem above board, and she had her own reasons for meaning to keep that promise. For a moment she was strongly tempted to turn round and go back now. But it was already almost five o'clock. She couldn't possibly get back before dark, and she was already tired from the long drive. Besides, the old man's hints may have been no more than those of the local who probably looked on anyone from farther than the next village as a foreigner and eccentric into the bargain. It was only fair to finish her journey, having come so far, and see for herself.

The lane was winding and climbed steeply between high banks topped with hedges, turning brown in the autumn sunshine. Linzi drove slowly, afraid that some other vehicle would come racing round one of the sharp bends towards her. She kept her windows down and heard the croak of a raven somewhere near at hand; in the banks she could see bracken, its fronds tinged with gold, and occasionally the scarlet berries of a rowan glowed like tiny lanterns in the hedge. The sky was a pale, tender blue, flecked with puffs of white cloud, and as the lane climbed higher and the banks fell away to give way to open hillside she saw the shoulder of the mountain ahead, its lower slopes still aflame with late gorse.

Linzi caught her breath. Well, if nothing else, it was worth coming just to see this! Whatever the situation at Bron Melyn, she just had to be grateful to the strange, unknown artist for bringing her here on this perfect autumn day. Even the roughness of the track as tarmac gave way to metalling didn't disturb her. The old man had said it would get rough, and there had been no side turnings for some way now. She must still be on the right road—and if not, when there were these views all round, who cared!

A few moments later, just when she was beginning to think that perhaps she had made a mistake somewhere, Linzi swung round a bend and found herself facing a house that seemed almost to be growing out of the hillside. Long, low, grey as the rocks that jutted from the hills, it looked strong enough to withstand any of the weather that winter might see fit to send—gale, blizzard, even a hurricane could not disturb its rugged serenity, Linzi felt as she stopped the car and sat staring at it. It looked a part of the mountain itself, with an air of slumbering power that awed and impressed her.

Behind it she could see a building that looked as if it might have been a barn, except that its slitted windows had been replaced with huge plate-glass. There were even windows in the roof, and Linzi, gazing at it, realised suddenly that this must be the artist's studio and, perhaps, gallery. She looked hastily at her map. There was no sign outside—at least, not one that she could see—but this, surely must be Bron Melyn.

A little doubtfully, she drove into the yard and pulled up. There didn't seem to be anyone about, but as she got out of the car and stood stiffly flexing her cramped muscles, the front door opened. A tall, thin man stood there, and as she glanced across he hurried forward.

'You must be Miss Berwick.' Linze nodded and opened her mouth, but before she could speak, he went on: 'I'm

Hugh—manservant, general factotum, chief cook and bottle-washer, dogsbody, call it what you will. Did you have any trouble finding us?'

'No, not really.' Linzi told him about the old man in Crickhowell, omitting the remarks which had caused him so much amusement. 'I hope you haven't been waiting for me?'

'Not at all. I was just worried in case you got lost.' He had a slight Welsh tang to his voice, she noticed, and wondered if he too were local. 'Look, you must be dying for a cup of tea. Come in and I'll make you one—I can bring your luggage in while you're having it, and put the car away for you too. It's a long drive down from London.'

He led the way into the house and Linzi followed, noting with appreciation the renovations that had changed this from what she guessed had been an old farmhouse to a tasteful and comfortable home. Natural wood complemented the old stonework, and plain glass let in light and set them both off. Shaggy Scandinavian rugs warmed the floor, catching the late afternoon sun as it slanted through the windows, and as she climbed the oak staircase Linzi saw that each window had its own wide-ranging view across the hills.

Hugh led her into a bedroom that brought a gasp of pure delight from her lips. It could, she thought as she paused for a moment on the threshold, have been decorated and furnished with herself especially in mind. Covering the floor was a thick moss-green carpet, its colour picked up in the Laura Ashley wallpaper and curtains. The duvet on the bed was covered with the same material, its white background giving a fresh, spacious feeling to the room. Fitted wardrobes lined one wall, with a dressing-table unit and full-length mirror lit by separate lamps. And through the large picture window opposite, Linzi could see a view of the whole valley stretching up away from the house, its rocky path climbing steadily beside a tumbling stream.

'There's your own bathroom and shower here, too,' Hugh explained, crossing to a door she hadn't noticed. 'So you're quite self-contained. Now, if you'd like a wash, everything's here, and I'll go down and make you some tea. Come down as soon as you're ready—the door on the right at the foot of the stairs.'

He turned to go, but Linzi, her curiosity suddenly too much for her, stopped him. She looked into his face, her topaz eyes gleaming with interest, and pushed back her golden-brown hair with an impatient hand. Her other hand lay lightly on his arm, slim and tanned against the pale blue sleeve of her shirt. For no reason at all, her heart had started to beat very fast.

'Please tell me,' she asked, feeling a quickening of her breath at the thought that at last she was about to know the answer, 'who *is* it I've come to work for? My agent wouldn't tell me—just said he was a well-known artist who hated publicity. But surely I can know now?'

She saw the hesitation in Hugh's eyes and stepped impulsively a little closer, intending to repeat her question. But even as she moved, Hugh's expression altered slightly. He seemed to be looking past her, and as she noticed this Linzi heard a sound out on the landing. Dropping her hand, she turned slowly round—and felt her body freeze.

Just beyond the door, in the semi-darkness of the landing, she could see the huge bulk of a man. He was standing perfectly still in the shadow and although she couldn't see his face, she knew he was watching her. And knew, with a sickening certainty, just what his expression must be. Cruel, harsh, unsmiling: craggy features set into a mask of disapproval, disapproval of her, as she'd so often seen them in the past. Black hair, falling forward over the high forehead, almost obscuring the brilliant blue eyes when it grew too long as it was sometimes allowed to do. A hard, muscular body, with not an ounce of fat for all its size; a frame that exuded a sense of power and dominance that went only too well, she realised, with this remote farm-house that stood with such confident arrogance in the Welsh hills, ready to withstand whatever storms might beset it.

Jason Carver. Jason, whose children she might have borne, who had tried all those years ago to dominate her. And he must hate her now as surely as he'd hated her then, when, filled with panic, she had run away and left him.

Why, after all this time, had he brought her here? *Was* it for the purpose he had given Anna to understand—that of artist's model? Or—more likely—was it for some cruel, subtle form of revenge?

CHAPTER TWO

FOR a long moment there was complete silence as Linzi and Jason stared at each other. Like a shadow, Hugh slipped past and down the stairs, leaving them alone. At the same moment, Jason moved forward into the light, his body filling the doorway.

Trying frantically to calm her thundering heart and quieten her rapid breathing, Linzi watched him. With a sudden odd pang she realised that he had aged in the five years since she had last seen him; his black hair was touched with a dusting of silver, his face even craggier with fresh lines etched upon it. But he was no less attractive for all that, she recognised unwillingly. The same magnetic power radiated from him, the same aura of essential masculinity seemed to emanate from his mere presence. He had become no less domineering, she was sure, and no less arrogant. He would still want his own way in everything. And she wondered, not for the first time, just how badly he had taken that knock to his ego dealt by her running away.

'Well.' He spoke at last, and Linzi closed her eyes. How often she had heard those deep tones in her thoughts and dreams! 'So we're together again at last. It's been a long time, Linzi.'

Linzi swallowed and whispered: 'Why have you brought me here? Why all the secrecy?'

'Would you have come without it?' he countered swiftly, and she was silent. 'Of course you wouldn't! You'd have run a thousand miles rather than face me.' He paused, then added with a menacing softness: 'Isn't that just what you did the first time?'

So it *was* revenge he was after! Linzi took a firm grip on herself and said in a low voice: 'Jason, that was five years ago. It's all in the past—over. If you've brought me here to——'

'I've brought you here for work,' he interrupted harshly. 'Didn't Anna tell you? I've a big commission, and I want you for it. Don't flatter yourself there was any other reason!'

Linzi sighed. Already he was having his usual effect on her. Already she was in the wrong, feeling herself accused of making false assumptions. Flatter herself indeed! She'd be grateful if it were just work that Jason Carver had on his mind—but she'd be surprised too. Whatever he said, she was going to tread very carefully indeed. In fact, she had half a mind to go straight downstairs, get into her car and drive back to London right away.

'I'm not *flattering* myself,' she retorted scathingly. 'Flattery hardly comes into it, does it? I'm sure you're not so hard up for women that you have to go to the lengths of bringing them down specially from London, without even daring to tell them who you are! I——'

She got no further. Jason had taken a stride that brought him close and before she could back away, he had her arms held with a cruel grip in huge, powerful hands. Linzi cried out and tried to wrench away, only to feel the iron fingers tighten so that she knew there must be bruises left on the tender skin. Her eyes filling with sudden tears, she gazed helplessly up at him, but found no mercy in the dark, glittering eyes.

'Let me go,' she whispered. 'You're hurting me!'

'If I am, it's no more than you deserve,' he grated, and let her go with a flick of his wrists that had her staggering. 'Don't try me too far, Linzi. I've taken all I'm prepared to take from you, so be warned. Any more remarks like that, and——'

He didn't finish, but he didn't have to. Linzi could feel enough animal power emanating from him to know that punishment would be swift and unforgettable. A tingle touched her spine as she thought what form that punishment might take; then she turned away, rubbing her wrists.

'All right,' she flung at him. 'So you want me to work for you. Couldn't you have said so in the first place? Don't I have *any* say in the matter—in what I do, where I go? If you thought I wouldn't come, knowing it was you, didn't it occur to you that I might leave just as soon as I found out?'

Jason smiled. Not the smile of devastating charm that she knew could touch his finely-chiselled lips and bring light to that dark face, but the sneering curl of the mouth that she feared and hated.

'Of course it occurred to me, my little rebel,' he murmured, 'that's why I insisted you sign a contract before you left London. I think I know you well enough to be sure that you won't go back on that. You wouldn't want to let Anna down, after all.'

Linzi turned back and stared at him. His eyes were cold and implacable. Was he saying that if she did leave he would *sue* her and Anna? Surely not! But, looking into those cold blue eyes, she wasn't so sure. The last five years seemed to have hardened him. And since she must, at least in part, have caused that hardening, there was no reason to suppose he would have any compunction in taking any steps he liked.

'You wouldn't do that,' she said slowly, her fingers still massaging her wrists. 'Not even to get back at me . . . Anna's never done a thing to harm you— why should she suffer?'

'No?' The eyebrow quirked again. 'She didn't exactly bend over backwards to help *me* when you took off five years ago, did she? Took you in—made a fuss of you— turned you into a top model. Without her, you might have seen sense, come back after you'd cooled down and saved a hell of a lot of trouble. Not that you'd have any idea what trouble you caused me—or care if you did. No, all you cared about was your spoilt, silly self.'

'That's not fair!' The tightly battened down emotions of five years threatened to break through as Linzi stared at him through a haze of tears. 'I wasn't ready for marriage—I realised that. And I knew you'd never listen if I told you how I felt. You'd already refused to let me go to college, or even away to work. You kept me on such a tight rein I hardly knew there *was* a world outside, let alone what it was like. I *had* to get away—and I had to do it secretly, because I knew you'd never let me go!'

'You're just rationalising!' His mouth was hard and angry, his eyes almost the colour of slate, their brilliance gone. 'Marriage was the only answer for us, and you knew it. After old Margery died and we were on our own, how else could we have gone on in the same house? And you were too young to be let loose——'

'I was, was I?' Linzi held up her hand so that he couldn't fail to see the thin gold wristwatch she wore, symbol of her success. 'But I managed to make my way, didn't I? *This* didn't come from being the failure you obviously expected me to be. Nor did my clothes, or my car, or my flat. Don't you think those just might prove you wrong, Mr Almighty?'

She panted into silence while his eyes assessed her coolly. The silence stretched out; Linzi's discomfort increased as he scrutinised her, his glance taking in every detail of her linen slacks, silk shirt and Italian shoes, the gold chain which encircled her neck, the leather belt that emphasised the slimness of her waist. Her heart thumped uncomfortably as his eyes left her body and met hers, holding them in an inscrutable stare that had a flush mounting in her cheeks. Speak, she wanted to say. Say *something*. But he still held the silence until, at last, he spoke in carefully measured tones, directly answering her last question.

'I wouldn't know,' he said, and the insult was unmistakable. 'After all, I don't know who bought them for you, do I—or under what circumstances.'

Linzi caught her breath. The implication was too plain for her to miss. Almost before she was aware of it, her hand had swung up and slapped Jason's cheek with a sharp crack that surely even Hugh must have heard. Immediately, aghast at what she'd done and terrified of his reaction, she took a step backwards, her golden eyes dark with apprehension. But Jason didn't move. He stood rigid, his muscles tense with the restraint he was all too clearly imposing, while the finger-marks blazed first white then red across his face.

'All right,' he said at last, and his voice was ragged. 'We'll forget you did that, shall we? At least for the time being. . . . But I've warned you once, Linzi. Next time you're going to be good and sorry, and don't you forget it.'

'Next time?' she repeated, her own voice shaking but still determined to hold her own against this tyrant. 'There won't *be* a next time, Jason. Didn't you understand what I said? I don't have to stay here—I don't have to do *anything* I don't want to do. I've made my own way in the world—reached the top of my profession, and without help from you or any other man.' She glanced again at the thin gold watch. 'Anything you see me wearing I bought myself—out of my own earnings. So you needn't forget I slapped your face, Jason. In fact, I'd rather you remembered it—just to remind you that I'm not the little Linzi you used to patronise. And as soon as you let me pass—and you'll have to move some time—I'll be down those stairs and into my car and away from you. And now I know where you are, *nothing* will get me back!'

She saw Jason's eyes widen as she spoke and knew with a stab of triumph that he was indeed seeing a new Linzi—not the little sister, eager to fetch and carry for him, but the woman she had become, confident and independent. And then the expression faded and the dark eyes narrowed to menace and, despite herself, she knew a pang of fear.

'And I made it clear to you,' he said slowly, his voice a low growl, 'that if you do that I'll be on to my lawyers before you've got as far as Crickhowell, instituting proceedings against you *and Anna* for breach of contract! I mean that, Linzi. And don't think it will all pass off unnoticed either. With a top modelling agent, one of her best models and Jason Carver involved, the story will make the front pages and gossip columns for months to come! And how will the up-and-coming banker like that, hey?'

'Richard!' Linzi's voice was a whisper. 'You know about Richard? And you—you'd drag *him* into it too?'

He uttered a short bark of scornful laughter. 'Of course I know about him! Your engagement didn't go unnoticed by the Press, you must know that. And I don't imagine this little bit of scandal would do his career a power of good, do you?'

Linzi turned away and stared out of the window. With every fibre of her body, every ounce of emotion, she longed to get away. To put as many miles as possible between her and Jason Carver; to push him once and for all right out of her life and her mind. But she knew that in this he had beaten her. It wouldn't be just Linzi Berwick who suffered if he carried out his threats, as she had not the slightest doubt he would do. Anna and Richard—the two people who meant most to her—their whole careers could be ruined. Jason was well aware of that; and he was having no compunction in using it to blackmail her into remaining here. With a tiny, hopeless shrug of her shoulders, she gave in.

'You seem to hold all the cards,' she said at last. 'All right, I'll sit for you. But we keep it strictly business. Nothing personal.'

'No?' One eyebrow went up in a quirk that was so familiar it twisted Linzi's heart. 'Not after all we've been to each other? Oh, I think that's being a little unrealistic, don't you?' Sinuously, almost imperceptibly, he had come closer and was now standing almost against her, so that when Linzi took a quick, involuntary breath, the points of her breasts brushed against his chest. She had to tilt her head to look up at him and as she did so she felt his hands on her arms again, gently this time but with an inherent firmness that told her his grip could tighten at her slightest move to escape.

'Nothing personal?' he murmured, his voice so low that she could feel its vibrations through her own body. 'Not even a kiss to say hello after such a long, long time apart . . .?'

Linzi's lips parted in silent protest, but before she could speak they had been claimed by the hard mouth that had only moments before curled in scorn. Panic leapt within her as she struggled in his arms, but their iron grip tightened around her and she felt herself crushed against his rock-like body. Taking no resistance as denial, his lips forced her own further apart, making a devastating exploration as she gasped for breath. One arm still holding her firmly against him, he let his other hand begin a journey over her slender waist and full curves. She felt his fingers fasten over her breast and knew that she could struggle no longer. Her senses were whirling as she let her own hands creep up round his neck, her fingers playing in the tumbled hair. Her lips moved with his as a wild flame of delight and desire ignited her body and she moved against him, whimpering at the intense longing that invaded and threatened to overwhelm her.

Slowly, almost reluctantly, his lips left hers and he drew away a little, still holding her, and looked down into her face. Linzi gazed up at him, breathing quickly, her eyes huge in her pale face. For a moment, the softness that had swept through her body was still there; then she saw the expression on his face and froze.

'Nothing personal, eh?' he mocked. 'That was just about the most *personal* kiss I've ever enjoyed—or is it your normal greeting to old friends? Maybe it is—you've been a long while away, and it seems you've found time to grow up.'

Linzi felt her face flame and twisted away from him. Her heart was thundering against her ribs again, but this time from anger. How dared he kiss her like that—waking up all sorts of unsuspected feelings—and then mock! And he knew just what he'd done to her, too, she mused bitterly. Knew exactly what response his lips and hands had called from her. Knew just how much he had aroused her.

'Don't do that again, or I *will* leave!' she spat at him. 'I don't think my contract covers *that* kind of co-operation. Any more of it, and I'm off!'

'Dear me,' he said silkily, 'we are the little wildcat, aren't we? Well, have it your own way, spitfire. I hereby promise I shan't touch you again—not unless you want me to, that is.' And he put out a finger and traced a delicate path from Linzi's cheek, down the slender neck and into the open collar of her shirt, keeping his eyes on hers as he did so. Linzi made a superhuman effort and kept quite still, trying to ignore the shivers that ran down her spine at his touch. She waited until he had removed his hand, then stepped away and said coolly:

'That'll be fine. We'll keep to that, shall we? Now, didn't Hugh say something about tea? It must be stewing by now, and I really would like some.'

Jason's eyebrows shot up at her coolness, then a touch of amusement quirked his lips as he said easily. 'Oh, Hugh won't let it stew. He'll make it as he hears us come downstairs. Would you like to follow me? Or do you want to wash your hands first?'

'Thank you, I'll wash,' Linzi said dismissively, and knew a tiny feeling of triumph as he turned and went out of the door. Almost as if she'd won that round, she thought exultantly; and then remembered that no one ever won in a battle with Jason Carver. . . .

Hugh had not yet brought her luggage upstairs—being tactful, no doubt, Linzi thought, and was grateful that he hadn't walked in on that scene with Jason—so she simply washed in the small but luxurious bathroom, and tidied her hair, brushing it to bring the chestnut gleam back after Jason's rough handling. Her pale blue shirt and matching slacks still looked neat, showing off her slim but curving figure to perfection, and she felt quite satisfied with herself as she looked in the mirror before turning to run downstairs.

Nevertheless, it wasn't that easy. The past half an hour or so had been a severe shock to Linzi. To find Jason Carver here, to realise that he was the mysterious 'artist', had awakened all kinds of unwanted memories and emotions. The two years between her father's death, only a few months after her mother's fatal car accident, and her eighteenth birthday, hadn't been easy ones. Left in Jason's care, she had at first been delighted; to have her idol to herself had seemed almost sufficient compensation for having lost both parents so young and so quickly. But Jason himself had soon dispelled any ideas she might have had about leaving school and living with him at the Cornish studio. He had insisted that she remain at school for a further two years, whereas Linzi had always intended to leave at the earliest possible moment. He had been more autocratic than any parent during the holidays, making her work at her holiday tasks and keeping a strict supervision of her leisure activities. Linzi, to her fury, had found herself always the one in any group who had to be home earliest; the one who was forced to leave the all-night parties before they'd properly begun, the one who had to ring home and report where she was if plans were changed, the one who had to take boys home to be approved before being allowed to make dates.

It was after one furious weekend of rebellion, when she had had a stand-up row with Jason and slammed out of the house to walk all night on the beach, that he finally suggested marriage.

Margery, the elderly housekeeper, had just died after a short illness. Linzi had been aware that Jason had been concerned about their situation, alone in the house, although it hadn't worried her. Her own adulation of him had disappeared since he had become so dictatorial, and her first reaction to his proposal was that he just wanted a cheap housekeeper. But he'd soon convinced her that that wasn't the case. No wife, he had told her with a rueful grin, had ever yet proved to be cheaper than a house-keeper!

'I've been thinking about this for quite a while,' he had told her as they looked out from the cottage window at the sand-dunes. 'We get along pretty well most of the time, we know each other through and through, and I know your parents would have been pleased. Look, I realise things haven't been easy for you, losing them both like that.' His face had twisted suddenly with pain. 'I loved them too, you know. They were mother and father to me as well. I miss 'em like hell, so I know just how you feel.'

It was that that had won Linzi's heart. Until that moment she had never seen the pain and grief that Jason had been bearing alone; too wrapped up in her own loss, she hadn't realised it had been his too. All her teenage love for him flooded back as she stared at the rugged face, its lines softened now by memories. Tentatively, she reached out and touched the rough cheek, traced a line down the strongly-jutting jaw. Jason was essentially a lonely person, she told herself, solitary as he worked all day in his studio with the harsh materials that were his trade. Perhaps he needed her. Just as she, restless and unhappy, needed him.

'All right, Jason,' she whispered, lifting her face for his kiss, 'I'll marry you.'

And he had kissed her, she remembered now, still poised on the top step of the stairs. But it hadn't been a kiss like the one he had given her not half an hour ago, the one that had brought a tingle to her spine, an urgent desire to her flesh. It had been tender, gentle, almost brotherly.

And it had left her strangely dissatisfied.

But all that would have to be forgotten now. If she were to get through this assignment—and pray heaven it wouldn't last too long—with any kind of dignity at all, the events of five years ago must never be allowed to surface, the emotions they awoke never be brought out into the open. To cope at all, she and Jason must remain on a cool, professional level; friendly because that was the only way to do it, but no more than that. For a heart-sinking moment she wondered if she would be able to go through with it; then she thought of Anna and Richard and knew that she must.

And before she could change her mind, she was on her way down.

The door on the right, Hugh had said. Taking a deep breath, Linzi opened the door and went in.

The first thing that met her eye was the view through the large sliding patio window, open now to the fresh warmth of the September evening, and looking up the same valley that she had seen from her bedroom. Outside was a terrace, with a table on which tea was set; as she crossed quickly to see the view more clearly, she realised that Jason was lying back in a garden chair near the table, and from his feet rose the golden-brown bulk of a large Alsatian dog.

'Don't worry, he won't attack,' came Jason's amused voice as Linzi hesitated. 'He'd like to shake hands, though. Then he'll know you're an accepted member of the household.'

And that's a joke, Linzi thought ruefully as she took the huge paw the dog offered her, feeling the roughness of his pads and the stiff hairs. The dog regarded her from dark brown eyes, then returned to his master and lay down again, still keeping his gaze fixed on her.

'All right, Bracken, it's a friend,' Jason told him. 'Come and have some tea, Linzi. It's all here—bara brith, Welsh cakes, scones and honey. Hugh's welcome for you.'

'It's very nice of him to go to so much trouble.' Linzi poured herself a cup of tea. 'Does he do all the cooking?'

'No, I have a go myself occasionally. But Hugh looks after things generally, though we do have a village woman for cleaning. Most of my time goes on my work, of course.' He glinted a look at her. 'I find it rather difficult to believe that you didn't at least suspect who the anonymous "artist" was, you know. You must have had at least half an idea.'

'I didn't! Not in the least!' Linzi retorted indignantly, then caught herself wondering if that were entirely true. Why else should Jason have impinged on her thoughts so much in the past few days, when she had thought her memories successfully buried? Was it some form of telepathy—that because he was arranging for her to come here, he came closer to her mind? Impatiently, she shrugged the idea aside. What nonsense—she'd been more aware of him simply because she was considering marriage, after having sworn that she never would again.

'I suppose I might have suspected if you'd used the word *sculptor* rather than artist,' she admitted thoughtfully. 'Presumably that's why you did it!' Indignation simmered again. 'I still think it was very underhand——'

'I've explained that.' His voice was abrupt. 'I knew you wouldn't come if you knew it was me, and I wanted *you*. Not for any—*personal*—reason, don't worry. But because for the commission I've got, you're exactly right. I'll show you why later.'

Linzi stared at him, fascinated. 'But how did you *know* I would be right? I might have changed—I might be completely different——'

'My dear child,' he said scathingly, 'do you think I didn't know exactly what you were like? Do you think I haven't known exactly where you were and what you were doing during the past five years? There was still that promise I made your father, you know. I've known just

when you were in London, when you were in Paris or
Rome. I knew when you went to New York and how well
you did there. I knew when you stopped spelling your
name Lindsey and called yourself Linzi. There's never
been a day when I haven't either known where you were
likely to be, or couldn't have found out.'

Linzi stared at him, feeling her body turn cold. All
those years she'd been trying to forget him, and he'd
known her every movement! Oh, not the details, she
realised that—it was just the broad outline of her life that
he referred to. But even so, she couldn't escape a feeling
of being trapped—hunted. Like a dog, let off the lead but
knowing that it could be called to heel at any moment.

'You—you've *watched* me, all that time?' she managed
at last. 'But why? Why?'

'Why? I've told you, I made a promise. I promised
your father on his deathbed that I'd look after you. I
don't break promises just because they become less easy
to keep.'

Linzi felt her face crimson as his glance raked her. It
was as if he was implying that she did just that—and she
knew that, from his point of view, she had. Could she
ever make him see that she had run away, not because
her promise was merely less easy to keep, but because it
was *impossible*? But she didn't want to get into that argument again. Instead she asked quickly:

'So you know all about me—and I know nothing about
you. What have you been doing?'

'Working,' he answered laconically. 'You obviously
haven't kept up with the art world—or my branch of it,
anyway. I suppose you could say I've made quite a name
for myself, with my sculpting. I've had several exhibitions,
anyway.'

She glanced at him from under her lashes, taking in the
signs of success—the suede slacks, the silk shirt in matching
dove grey, the thin gold chain that glinted among the
hairs of his chest, and the answering dull gleam from his

Longines wristwatch. Catching his sardonic glance, she looked hastily away, searching for a distraction, and at the end of the terrace saw a tall slab of marble, smoothed to the texture of satin and glowing with a translucency that turned to amber in the warmth of the evening sun. An example of his work? she wondered. Jason followed her gaze and nodded.

'I brought that piece of marble back from Italy. It's my favourite—I don't think I'll ever sell it.'

Linzi glanced at him in quick surprise at the sentiment. But Jason had never been entirely hard, she recalled. He'd been deeply fond of her own parents—fond enough to consider a deathbed promise totally binding, even when it threatened to interfere with his own life. It was only towards herself that he had been so implacable. . . .

'When did you come to live in Wales?' she asked, shying away from the questions that kept raising themselves in her mind. 'The last I heard you were in Cornwall.' It was vivid in her own memories, the studio Jason had had in the north Cornish fishing village near St Ives. He had moved there when she was only twelve, and she recalled holidays spent there with her parents. Long, sunlit days when they'd fished and swum and sailed; days when she had sat for hours in the studio, watching with absorbed attention as Jason chipped painstakingly away at his slabs of rock, gradually etching out a shape that was so right for each individual stone it was as if it had always been there, hidden inside, waiting only for the right eyes to see it and the right hands to set it free. And Jason had those eyes and hands. Even as a small boy he had had them; and he had been fortunate, as he had always been the first to acknowledge, that after his own parents' deaths when he was only three years old, the Berwicks had taken him in and recognised his potential as soon as it began to emerge.

Linzi hadn't been born then; she had arrived twelve years later, when Robert and Elizabeth Berwick had given up all hope of having children of their own. But she knew that from the first they had treated Jason, child of one of Robert's old school friends, as their own. She knew that they had done all they could to encourage his development as a woodcarver and sculptor, sending him to the best art colleges both in England and abroad to study.

And to give him credit, Jason had never forgotten his debt to them. He had been away most of the time by the time Linzi was old enough to notice his presence. But his visits home had been frequent enough for him to become her idol. And he had treated her in a fond, rather patronising way as his younger sister, letting her watch him at work, using her as a willing slave just as any elder brother might do. It was only later that things had changed. . . .

'I've been here for three years now,' he answered her question. 'Inherited the place from that old uncle of mine—Walter. He was too old ever to take much notice of me when I was a child—he was my great-uncle really— but he always said he'd do what he could for me. Couldn't afford it while he was alive, poor old chap—but I blessed him for Bron Melyn when he died.'

'But you loved Cornwall!' Linzi had loved it too—the atmosphere in nearby St Ives, where so many artists gathered and Jason's own idol, Barbara Hepworth, had had her own studio. She remembered seeing huge slabs of marble and granite being manhandled through the tiny cobbled streets; raw material, its secrets still locked inside it; and later the completed sculptures destined for the parks and gardens, the colleges and the great buildings they were to enhance.

Jason shrugged. 'Yes, I loved it. But—things changed.' He was staring up the valley, his brilliant eyes veiled by the heavy lids and dark lashes. 'And when Bron Melyn came along I knew it was right for me to come here. And so it has been. I've done my best work here.' His glance wandered to the marble slab, so plainly done, a single form with a slash of gold across it where the sun speared its last rays through a notch in the hills. It was different every time you looked at it, Linzi thought, fascinated; already she was looking forward to her first view of it in the morning. She was sure that Jason would have placed it just where it could draw the most from its environment.

'I'll show you the studio if you've had enough tea,' he said abruptly. 'Hugh will be wanting us in for dinner at eight—I always eat then, when I've finished work for the day—and I suppose you'll be wanting to change before that.' His glance skimmed over her and Linzi felt suddenly scruffy, even though only half an hour earlier she had felt perfectly satisfied with her appearance. Before she could speak, he was on his feet, with the litheness of a panther in his spring, and walking away towards the barn without a backward glance, followed closely by Bracken.

Presumably she was expected to follow him too! Linzi felt indignation bubble inside her again. Once upon a time she would have conceded weakly to this treatment, thrilled that he even noticed her presence—but that was years ago. She was grown up now, she told herself savagely as she got to her feet and walked after him, deliberately taking her time. Not an adoring child, nor even a lovesick teenager, but a woman. . . . And the thought of his kisses burned across her memory again, so that she turned hot and had to pause for a moment to regain control of her suddenly hammering heart.

Was it because she'd grown up that Jason Carver's kisses affected her in this way? There had been nothing like it during their earlier relationship—even during their brief engagement. Was that part of the reason why she had run away from him then, the unformulated knowledge that something vital was missing? And if so, what did its emergence now mean, to either of them?

Jason had reached the door of the barn and turned impatiently to see where she was. For a moment Linzi stood quite still, seeing him in an entirely new light. Not as the beloved idol of her childhood; not as the man from whom she had escaped only days before a wedding that terrified her; nor even as the domineering male who had assaulted her senses as soon as she had met him, waking a sensuality she hadn't known existed in herself.

But as some strange figure of doom; an almost mythical being, with the power to shape her life as he shaped the rocks around them. A god of bronze and marble, in whose hands she, like the stone he wrought to suit his own purposes, was totally helpless.

'For heaven's sake,' Jason said impatiently as she reached him at last, 'you looked as if you'd been turned to stone, standing there. What's the matter—caught sight of my pet basilisk?'

'Your pet——?' For a moment, still shaken by her vision, she didn't understand. Then she remembered the childhood joke she had once made when in his Cornish studio: that he had only pretended to sculpt the figures that stood about on their plinths, that in fact they were locals 'looked on' by a basilisk he kept hidden nearby, and so turned to stone. It surprised her that he should have remembered it; but she smiled as best she could, thankful for the help it gave her now in recovering from a moment that had troubled her more than she cared to admit.

Jason opened the door of the barn and led the way inside. The sun had almost disappeared now; the great space was filled with a blue-grey twilight. They stood at the entrance together, looking into the gloom. Linzi saw the dim shapes gradually form; shapes that loomed out of the impending darkness, strange and menacing. Then Jason reached out and flicked down the light switch, and she gasped, momentarily dazzled.

The light came from long fluorescent tubes, reflecting off the pure white walls. There was light everywhere, it seemed. It was essential, Jason had once explained to her, to have a light studio. Light was important to sculpture; you couldn't see the shapes in a bad light, couldn't tell exactly what you were doing. Imperfections and roughnesses could go unnoticed.

Her eyes growing used to the glare, Linzi looked around. The barn was completely renovated inside and formed one large, high room—high enough for the tallest sculpture, its great doors wide enough for the bulkiest to pass through. The large windows in walls and roof would let in enough natural daylight when the sun shone; on dark winter days and during the night the fluorescent tubes would take over.

At one end of the studio she saw Jason's workbench, running the full width and covered with tools, maquettes and small pieces in various stages of completion. The studio was well heated too, she noticed, with electric storage heaters; there must be no risk of damage to the work during cold weather.

The rest of the space was taken up with Jason's gallery—sculptures of all sizes, ranged some on shelves, some on plinths. Fully absorbed, she wandered away from his side, examining them. Many of them she would have recognised as being Jason's work, simply from her knowledge of his work in Cornwall. Others were of styles new to her. Fascinated, she gazed at the busts, heads and full-size figures, both animal and human; wondered at the life and vitality that seemed to shimmer from the cold stone and metal. She could almost see the muscles of a great bull ripple as she approached him; almost flinched at the violence expressed in the tension of a boxing champion's stance. But other pieces were less easy to understand. Slabs of bronze or marble, asymetrical in shape, with holes in odd places; what did they mean? Figures that were—or were they?—surely meant to represent the human figure, standing, kneeling, reclining, also with strange holes. And others that meant nothing at all to her in shape, yet seemed to suggest something she could not put into words and drew her to touch, tentatively, their flowing curves and to rest her hands in their hollows or to cup their rounded arches.

At last she turned and walked slowly back to where Jason was standing by the door, watching her. His expression was closed and enigmatic; perhaps he too had his memories of those days in Cornwall. He said nothing as she approached.

Hesitantly, Linzi remarked: 'You—you seem to have moved on a lot since I last saw your work, Jason. Some of it I would have known anywhere as yours. But the rest——' She finished her words with a shrug.

He nodded, but evidently wasn't disposed to talk about it. His work had always been too precious to him for idle chatter, she remembered, and tried to not feel sad at the thought that once she had been one of the few he was willing to discuss it with.

'What kind of thing is it you want me for?' she enquired, wondering now if the finished work would, after all, resemble her in any way.

Jason grinned, obviously reading her thoughts. 'Don't worry, you're not going to end up as a slab of marble with a hole in the middle!' He crossed to a drawing-board which stood at one side, near the workbench. 'Look, these are a few preliminary sketches. See, it'll be in bronze—very large, about twenty feet high—very *airy*-looking. I suppose the nearest way to describe it is a kind of modern-style figurehead, like they used to have on ships. A symbol of progress and forward-looking success. Life, forging ahead—get the idea?'

Linzi did. Staring at the sketches in fascination, she asked: 'And you think I can convey that?' It took some assimilating, the idea that Jason should even have considered her for such a role.

'Yes. Your looks are just right, and you still have that air of eagerness, an excitement in life that's always been the most attractive thing about you.' He spoke in an unemotional, even professional tone that had nothing to do with the way his words brought colour to her cheeks. 'I was afraid that might have gone—and it's that that I need most of all. It brings a certain tension to your entire body, your whole attitude and posture, that's exactly the spirit of what I want to portray. Lose that and it'll fall completely flat.' He turned suddenly from the drawing and looked down at her, eyes brilliant again under the stark lighting. 'So don't lose it, Linzi—at least not while you're here.'

Not much chance of her losing it, if it was tension he was talking about, Linzi thought. She was like a tightly-wound spring! But she merely nodded and shifted away slightly, pretending an extra interest in the drawings. 'And where's this figure going to go?'

'Over the entrance of that new hotel they're building in London,' Jason answered. 'The Berkeley Palace.' His eyes glinted in appreciation of her reaction. 'You'll really stun 'em there, Linzi. It's a big thing for us both if it succeeds—and it's my intention that it should!'

Linzi shook her head slowly. She had known this was an important commission, but she had never dreamed that it might result in her likeness adorning the façade of one of the most prestigious hotels in London—a hotel that, even before building had started, had excited more comment than any other. She remembered her feeling that this assignment might prove to be something more worthwhile than anything she had yet done, and wondered how Richard would react when he knew. Not much of the furtive and distasteful about *this*, in spite of his worries!

'Well?' Jason asked softly. 'Does the idea appeal? Or do you still want to go back?'

Linzi forgot all their previous animosity, all the doubts and fears and all the dread she had felt when she had discovered that it was he who had brought her here. She turned a shining face on him, a face which glowed with excitement and pride, with eyes that were incandescent as flame.

'Appeal?' she repeated. 'I've never ever dreamed that I'd be asked to do anything like this. It's the most marvellous thing that's ever happened. Thank you for thinking of me, Jason.'

She took a step forward, lifting her face for an impulsive kiss, just as she would have given to anyone who had given her such pleasure. But even as she raised herself on tiptoe, something stopped her and made her draw back. Jason hadn't moved—but his expression, closed again and totally unreadable, hit her like a blow. Her kiss wouldn't be welcomed, she realised as she sank back again. Neither would her gratitude. As she herself had asserted, this was to be a strictly professional, business relationship. And, curiously deflated, she turned away towards the door.

'I'll be ready to start work whenever you like in the morning,' she said in a low voice, and knew from the tiny sound that escaped Jason's lips that he was satisfied.

Over dinner, they talked desultorily about things that kept them off personal details, things that they could discuss without emotion. And soon after coffee, Linzi said she was tired after the long drive and would like to unpack now and go to bed. Jason made no demur as she stood up, and didn't move from his own armchair, even when she stooped to pat Bracken goodnight. She climbed the oak stairs slowly, conscious of an intense weariness, a weariness that came from more than a long drive, but from emotional unheaval, shock and a strangely exhilarating excitement as well.

And still, she reflected when she had finished her unpacking and was sitting in the window-seat of the bedroom gazing up the darkened valley, she wasn't entirely sure why Jason had brought her here. Was it simply for the bronze figure, as he'd said? Or was there some other, more sinister reason . . .?

CHAPTER THREE

DURING the next few days Linzi found herself settling down at Bron Melyn, though her thoughts and feelings were still in some turmoil. It was strange, after all this time, to be in daily contact with Jason again. There was an odd, painful familiarity about sharing meals with him; sitting in the same room, often without talking; hearing him move around the house or watching him cross the yard to the studio. It was all so well known that she sometimes wondered if the past five years had been no more than figment of her imagination; if she had dreamed them and somehow lost her memory of how they had really been. The thought gave her a jolt, almost as if she half believed it; then she shook herself and mentally took herself to task for being over-imaginative.

But if being with Jason was painfully familiar, there was also much that was strange. He had changed subtly during those years, she thought, developed the strength and maturity that had been budding during his twenties when, after long years of study, he had returned to England and set up that first studio in Cornwall. He was now in his prime, both as a man and as a sculptor. And, not for the first time, Linzi wondered just what her life might have been if she had not run away—if she had stayed, and married him. By now, they might have acknowledged their mistake and been parted, for ever this time. On the other hand. . . .

But it did no good at all to think along those lines. No good to dwell on Jason's firm lips, or feel again the pressure of them on her own. No good to visualise again his hard, muscular body, the powerful arms and wrists that were accustomed to handling heavy weights, slabs of granite and marble, yet could be so tender around a woman's body; to watch those long hands and remember that they were as sensitive when they carved a form from rock or wood as when they moved sensuously over her breast.

Linzi moved impatiently and went to stare out of her bedroom window. It was still early in the morning. A haze hid the valley and hills, giving a soft golden glow to the landscape as the sun rose behind the house. A movement from below caught her attention and she saw Jason let himself out of the door, Bracken bounding beside him. The pair of them set off up the valley, oddly alike as they swung, loose-limbed and full of vibrant energy, up the rocky path.

This afternoon, Linzi promised herself, she too would go for a walk up the valley. So far, there hadn't been time. Mornings had been spent in the studio, working with Jason. There was a good deal to do before he actually began the clay model that would be the first stage of the actual sculpture. He was making preliminary drawings and maquettes of her head and limbs. He spent a good deal of time just studying her; asking her for different poses, considering her from all angles. It was curiously intimate, yet Linzi felt no embarrassment. In the studio, they were both professionals. Personal relationships didn't enter into the work they were doing together. It was only away from the old barn with its brilliant lights, its gallery of sculpture and its long workbench, that any strain began to come between them.

Linzi went into her bathroom to shower, dressing afterwards in the leotard Jason had asked her to wear for work and covering up with jeans and a checked shirt. The final figure was to show her in loose, flowing robes, but Jason was concerned to get the shape underneath before going on to that stage. He said there was no way he could imply what was underneath without actually knowing and building up from that, and Linzi understood this.

Hugh had just finished setting breakfast when she went down. They were still eating as many meals as possible out on the terrace—September had proved to be unexpectedly warm, an Indian summer after the usual poor English—or Welsh—one. Linzi went out through the patio door, smiling a good-morning at Hugh, and sat down, resting her elbows on the table as she gazed up the valley.

'You're settling in all right, are you, Miss Berwick?' Hugh asked. 'Jason seems to be very pleased with the way things are going so far.'

'Yes, I think the work's progressing. And I must admit I love Bron Melyn—it's so peaceful and beautiful.' She let her eyes rove over the solid, grey building set so firmly in the side of the hill. 'I keep meaning to ask, Hugh—what does the name mean?'

'It means yellow hillside.' He nodded up the valley, where the smooth slopes of the hill were golden with gorse still. Higher up, the mountain was craggier and purple with heather, the soft amethyst colour merging into the white-flecked blue of the morning sky. Linzi let her eyes rove over the horizon to the shadows of more distant hills, and felt a sudden need to get up there, roam amongst the heather and gorse, to be entirely alone with the rocks and tumbling streams. So far, she had been too tired after the morning's work to think of going far. But today, having become accustomed to the routine, she felt refreshed and ready to tackle something more strenuous.

'There's Jason,' Hugh remarked suddenly. 'Bracken's had a good walk, by the look of him. That'll keep him settled for the rest of the day.'

'How long has Jason had Bracken?' Linzi asked idly. She had grown used to the huge Alsatian shadowing Jason wherever he went, and had begun to make friends with him.

'Two years. He was a police dog, but he had a bad accident—got run down by a motorbike when he was chasing some young thugs in Newport. He had to have an operation and after that he was declared unfit for police work and retired. He hasn't forgotten his training, though.' They both watched as the dog bounded down the last part of the track towards them. 'Jason makes sure he still remembers about keeping to heel when necessary, and all that sort of thing. And he's a marvellous tracker.'

He passed Linzi a bowl of grapefruit and she began to eat while he went to fetch coffee. Jason arrived as she poured her first cup, and she glanced at him, thinking how fresh and healthy he looked after his morning walk. He was wearing well-cut jeans today and a dark blue shirt that opened to show his strong, tanned throat and the dark hairs that curled on his chest. He fitted in with the landscape, she thought suddenly; the strength and power that emanated from him seemed to radiate from the mountains as well. It was a landscape of moods—so far she had only seen it in its sunnier frame of mind, but she knew that there must be times when these mountains were threatening and dark, when the valleys offered little comfort and the rocks gave little shelter. And Jason could be just as frightening, she knew; and shivered as she thought once again that she must not be lulled by the beauty of this gentle September. There was menace under the golden surface; thrilled and excited as she was by the assignment, she must remember that once it was at an end Bron Melyn must be put behind her, for good. She had another life to return to, and nothing must put that at risk.

Her thoughts brought Richard to her mind and she determined that today she must try to telephone him. She had written the day after she had arrived, of course, but there was no knowing whether he had received her letter. And he might still not even know where she was.

'Do you mind if I use the phone later?' she asked Jason. 'I'll pay for the call, of course—it will be a foreign one, probably to Germany.'

Jason raised his eyebrows. 'But of course. This will be to the banker, I take it? Did you say he was in Europe at present?'

'Yes,' Linzi said shortly, annoyed by the faintly mocking tone. 'He's on a business trip. Otherwise I wouldn't have been able to come here, of course.'

'No?'

'No,' she answered sharply. 'If Richard hadn't been going abroad, we would probably have brought our wedding forward. There certainly wouldn't have been time for long assignments in the Welsh mountains, even for the famous Jason Carver.'

'Ah, I see.' His tone was still patronising, and Linzi seethed. 'Of course. Even the famous Jason Carver must take second place to the highly successful Richard Fabian, mustn't he?'

Linzi looked up and met his eyes. There had been more in that comment than the words alone implied. Tension crackled between them as Hugh appeared with a plate of bacon and eggs for Jason and toast for Linzi. When he had gone, she leaned forward a little and answered the deliberately provocative remark.

'Yes,' she said quietly, 'he certainly must. In fact, he always has.'

She held Jason's blue eyes with her own golden-brown ones, and knew that the shaft had gone home. Jason could be in no doubt now that she considered him second-best— in every way. In life—and in love.

There was a moment's silence. Jason slowly finished his grapefruit, his eyes studying her from under beetling brows. They seemed to look right through her, to strip her of all pretence, to lay bare the real Linzi who trembled in confusion beneath the cool veneer. He'll know more about me than I do myself, she thought wildly, and that seemed indeed to be Jason's opinion too, for after a moment he withdrew his gaze as if satisfied, and reached for his bacon and eggs.

'That's fine, then,' he said noncommittally. 'By the way, I'd like to get started early this morning if that's all right by you. I've got the foundryman coming later on for some preliminary discussions. Say in half an hour?'

'Yes, I'll be ready,' she murmured, oddly shaken by the mute encounter that had seemed to be almost a touching of mind to mind. She finished her coffee. 'I'll see you then.'

For a moment she hesitated, half expecting Jason to detain her in some way. But he merely nodded as he began to slice his bacon, and she went indoors feeling strangely blank.

Herr Fabian had already left for his meeting, the receptionist in the German hotel told her when Linzi finally got through. He would be back in the evening and would be given her message then, and no doubt he would ring her back.

Linzi replaced the receiver and turned to see Megan coming through the door, ready to start her morning's cleaning. They smiled at each other; already they had become friends, though there hadn't been much time for talking, as Megan had often already left the house when Jason called a halt to the morning's work. But Linzi instinctively liked the dumpy little Welshwoman; she enjoyed listening to the musical lilt of her voice and had made up her mind that some day she would find time for a good gossip about the mountains that were beginning to take such a grip on her imagination.

'A lovely morning it is, again,' Megan remarked, putting her coat away and wrapping herself in the overall she used for work. 'I like it to be nice in September. Shortens the winter, see.'

'I suppose winters can be very bleak here,' said Linzi, glancing through the window at the bulk of the hills. 'Do you get much snow?'

'Oh, we get our share.' Megan began to sort through

brooms and dusters. 'Starts early sometimes, too. When it's raining down in Abergavenny, or Monmouth, it's snowing up here. You want to be careful up on them old hills then, Miss Berwick. The weather can change while you blink, and it's never for the better. Don't go up there on your own, look.'

'Oh, I shan't be here then. I'll be going back to London as soon as Mr Carver's finished with me.' Not the best phrase to use, she thought ruefully, but Megan seemed unaware of any undertones.

'Yes, I suppose you will.' To Linzi's surprise, Megan sounded almost regretful. 'Seems funny, that, but you've fitted in here so well. Like as if you belonged, in a way. Not like . . . oh well.' She turned away, busying herself with the vacuum cleaner.

'Not like who?' Linzi asked curiously, and Megan hesitated, her round face a little flushed. 'Has Mr Carver had other models staying here?' No reason why he shouldn't, and she'd certainly seen sculptures of the female figure in the studio that must have been done from life. She remembered one head in particular—a small, neat head with pretty features, short, curling hair and, even in bronze, a flirtatious look about the eyes.

'Not staying, no. You're the first he's had in the house. No, I wasn't meaning a model, Miss Berwick.' She hesitated again and Linzi waited, half ashamed of herself for encouraging Megan to gossip about her employer, yet too intrigued to want to stop her. But before Megan could speak again, Jason himself came through the hall. Megan immediately turned away, her cheeks more rosily flushed than ever, and Linzi sighed a little and moved towards the stairs.

'Almost ready?' Jason asked abruptly, watching her as she began to go up. 'I want to get quite a bit done this morning before Prosser arrives.'

'Yes, I'm almost ready—I'll be right down.' And Linzi, still acutely conscious of the eyes that followed her to the top of the open staircase, ran lightly to the top and, thankfully, into her own room.

Why was it that Jason Carver could *always* make her feel in the wrong? If only he knew that she was every bit as anxious as he that the work should be finished as quickly as possible—so that she could get away from this dangerous place, and back to the safety of London and Richard's affectionate but undemanding arms.

The sun was high as Linzi, dressed again in jeans and T-shirt, set off up the valley on the walk she had promised herself. Lunch had been early, letting Jason get back to the studio as soon as Mr Prosser, the foundryman, had arrived to discuss the sculpture. There would be other such talks, Jason had told her; he liked the foundryman to be in right from the start so that no unforeseen snags might occur. The figure was to be made in silicon bronze, for extra strength and lightness, and both this and other technicalities, like the invested mould, master cast and roman joints, all had to be discussed. It was all beyond Linzi and she was glad to leave them to it, although Alun, the young man from Crickhowell who looked after the garden and helped Jason with the hard labour that was so much involved in sculpture, was already hanging on their every word.

Outside in the lane the hedges were heavy with ripe blackberries, and Linzi picked a few as she walked along, wondering if either Hugh or Megan would use them to make jam. Her mother had often made blackberry and apple jam in the autumn. . . . After a few hundred yards, however, the hedges stopped abruptly and Linzi found herself crossing a cattle grid on to the open hillside. And here the terrain was quite different; open moorland, dotted with gorse bushes, and populated by fleecy sheep with black noses, grazing the short springy turf.

The stream that ran past the house chattered its way down beside the track, creating tiny waterfalls as it slid over rounded boulders brought down by rain and flood. Linzi watched it as she went, noting the mosses and ferns that grew at its edges. She heard a croaking cough from above and looked up quickly to see a large black bird flapping overhead. A raven, probably. And that further speck, wheeling so high and seeming to use its wings more to glide than to fly, must be a buzzard.

She was high above the house by the time she turned to look back, and it was strange to see it laid out below her, almost like a child's toy. She watched for a while, seeing Hugh come out from the kitchen door and cross to the vegetable garden; thinking of tonight's dinner, no doubt. Then Alun left the studio, followed after a while by Jason and Mr Prosser, who stood gazing at the doors and yard before going back in again. Considering how to get the figure out, she thought, and realised suddenly what the old man in Crickhowell had meant by 'games' and 'all sorts' going up the track. Of course, it must be quite a spectacle sometimes to see a large, unwieldy sculpture being transported away from such a remote spot. And she remembered again seeing those great figures being man-handled through the streets of St Ives from Barbara Hepworth's studio.

Turning, Linzi continued on her way up the valley. She was nearing the top now, and eager to see what lay beyond. As she could have guessed, it was another hill—but as she stood there, the cool breeze lifting her hair, she was suddenly overwhelmed by a feeling of pure belonging; as if this were indeed her place, the place where she was meant to be. The wild mountains stretched ahead of her—rounded, flat-topped, conical. She wanted to explore them all, know all their tracks and ways, and not just in summer either. She imagined them in snow, in thunder and hail, and a strange excitement pervaded her body and tingled through her limbs. It was almost like the ex-citement she'd felt when Jason had kissed her, she thought—and groaned a little at the memory. Why did he have to force his way in everywhere? Couldn't she be free of him, just for one afternoon?

Linzi sat down on a smooth rock near the edge of the stream. Maybe it would be better if she *did* let the memories come back? If she took them òut and looked at them, they might cease to torment her. After all, she was a different person now. Five years older and—surely— wiser. She might find that she'd been running from shadows all this time.

For the first time for years she let the morning she had run away from Jason come to the forefront of her mind. It wasn't easy—for a long time she had been pushing it back, afraid of the pain it could cause her. But now, taking a firm grip on herself, she forced herself to remember— everything.

The first few days after Jason had proposed had been heaven. All her unhappy tension seemed to have evaporated and she realised that it had been caused largely by insecurity—an insecurity that had begun with her mother's death and come to a head with her father's last illness. Without either of them, she was like a boat with neither rudder nor anchor, drifting helplessly. And the anchor Jason had tried to provide had been too strong her, dragging her under as she floundered desperately to find her own depth.

Engaged to him, wearing the pearl ring that had been his own mother's engagement ring, she had felt secure for the first time for over two years. But it had been all too short a reassurance.

She remembered the day the doubts had first begun to creep in. She had been with a girl from the group she usually spent her free time with, although the girl her- self—Cindy—wasn't one of Linzi's close friends. They had met on the beach and were wandering along together, discussing Linzi's engagement and wedding.

'Will it be a white one?' Cindy asked and, without waiting for an answer: 'I must say, we were all bowled over by the news. My mother says she never thought Jason *would* marry. A bachelor gay, that's what she called him!'

'What do you mean?' Linzi stopped and stared at her.

'Oh, you know—plenty of girls, plenty of fun, nothing serious. Well, I suppose you wouldn't know—you've been away most of the time. But he hasn't lived like a monk, as they say!' And Cindy giggled meaningly.

Linzi said nothing. She should have realised, she told herself, that Jason would have had girl-friends. But none of them had been in evidence while she was there, and somehow she'd never thought about it. Anyway, it wasn't important—*she* was the one he was marrying. And she changed the subject to Cindy's own current love-life, a subject of even more absorbing interest to that young lady.

But later, the doubts returned. Linzi stood in front of her mirror, staring at the lanky, gawky reflection; lifted the heavy mop of chestnut hair. What could a man like Jason Carver, almost twice her age, see in her? She had told herself he loved her—he must love her, or why else should he be marrying her? And to her dismay there was an answer already in her mind. It was because of that promise he had made to her father—the promise that he would look after her. It was because he had come to the conclusion that marriage was the only way in which he could control her. Love—other than the brother-sister affection they had shared for years—just didn't come into it.

Once that thought had entered her mind, Linzi found it impossible to get it out. Vainly she sought for proof that Jason *did* love her. But his affection was as casual as ever. His kisses were tender, but passionless. And in the end, convinced that she was right but knowing he would never admit it or let her go to make her own life, she had panicked. She had realised, blindingly, that however much she loved him, a marriage of this kind could never work, could only result in heartbreak. And with a clear, cruel self-knowledge, she had admitted that she just wasn't mature enough to cope with the problems it would bring. She needed to get away—needed time and space to grow up.

She had slipped out one morning after he had gone to the studio, knowing that he wouldn't appear again until lunchtime. And by then, she would be far away; swallowed up in the anonymous crowds of London.

It had been more than fortunate, she thought now, knowing some of the things that could have happened to an entirely inexperienced girl arriving in such circumstances, that she had remembered her old school house-captain, Anna. Otherwise she might well have been going home with her tail between her legs a week or two later. Or even worse. . . .

'So this is where you've got to!' Linzi started violently and looked up with a feeling of inevitability at the tall figure that loomed above her. 'Hugh told me you'd come up here. But he wouldn't have known if he hadn't seen you on the track. I suppose it didn't occur to you to let anyone know where you were going?'

'No, as a matter of fact it didn't,' Linzi retorted heatedly. 'Why should it? I understood that afternoons were my free time, unless you'd made some arrangement beforehand.'

Jason sighed and coiled his lithe body down on the rock beside her. 'It's nothing to do with hours or afternoons off,' he told her. 'It's a question of safety. You don't know these hills at all, yet you come wandering up here alone without giving anyone any idea of which direction you mean to take—without any proper footwear or protective clothing in case the weather changes,' he added with a derisive glance at her T-shirt and light walking shoes, 'and, I'm quite certain, without any such thing as a compass—I don't suppose you even know how to use one. This isn't Hyde Park, you know. This is wild country—if you don't know what you're doing, you can find yourself in trouble, and I mean trouble. Or maybe you fancy the idea of lying out in the heather all night with a sprained ankle until someone happens to find you. *If* they do.'

Linzi bit her lip. She had to admit that his words made sense—yet, looking around the pleasant hillside with its gold and purple clothing, she could hardly believe that it was as dangerous as Jason made out. Surely he was just putting her into the wrong again—or trying to. She tossed back her tawny hair and scrambled to her feet.

'Well, it looks safe enough to me,' she declared. 'There's not a cloud to be seen, it's as warm as July, and the track's plain to be seen. So if you don't mind, I think I'll continue my walk.'

'I don't mind at all.' Jason came lazily up to stand beside her. 'I'll come with you.' And when she opened her mouth to protest, he added harshly: 'I'm not listening to any arguments, Linzi. You're *not* used to these hills, and until you are I don't want you coming up here alone. And before you come up again, anyway, I want you wearing proper boots and carrying at least an anorak. And that's an order!'

Linzi stared at him, her eyes stormy. But his face was about as tractable as a granite cliff. With a gasp of exasperation and another toss of her head, she turned away abruptly and began to walk quickly up the track.

Jason fell into step beside her and she became aware of Bracken loping alongside, sometimes drawing ahead, sometimes pausing to wait, his tongue lolling out in a wide grin of pleasure at this extra walk. They walked in silence for a while. Linzi told herself angrily that she might as well go home; her pleasure in the afternoon had been utterly spoilt by Jason's interference. But the beauty of the hills was too much for her bad temper, and after a while she found herself relaxing again, able to enjoy the clear, bracing air and the colours all around her. She glanced sideways at Jason and caught him doing the same.

His mouth widened in a reluctant grin, and she felt her own twitch in answer, and suddenly the tension eased and they were smiling at each other naturally for the first time since she had arrived.

'Marvellous, isn't it?' Jason remarked, spreading his arms to include the whole wide vista of mountain and moorland. 'There hasn't been a day go by that I haven't thanked Uncle Walter for leaving me Bron Melyn. Oh, it might not be the ideal place as far as work's concerned, in one way—we have terrible problems getting the bigger pieces down the track, and the raw material up it. But in other ways, it couldn't be better. And as a place to live. . . .' His silence spoke louder than any words could have done. Linzi glanced at him with complete sympathy.

'I know,' she agreed. 'It's wonderful. I'm dreading the day I have to leave—from that point of view,' she added hastily as she caught his quizzical look.

'Of course,' he agreed gravely. 'But you wouldn't really like to live here, Linzi. You've only seen it in its more peaceful, benevolent moments. The Black Mountains can be cruel, you know. Harsh in winter. Not the kind of life you'd enjoy at all.'

'Why not?' Linzi was unaccountably stung by his words. Dimly, she felt that Jason ought to have known her better than that—ought to have remembered her love for the outdoor life, her deep interest in country things. Probably he thought she had left all that behind during her years as a model. But there had been times, when modelling clothes at fashion shows in Paris or enduring hot and seemingly endless photographic sessions in New York, that she had longed to be out in the country again, swinging along just as she was now on a mountain track, or strolling through some deep green lane. 'I haven't changed that much, you know.'

'No?' His blue eyes were speculative. 'But surely you're committing yourself to a city life? Once you're married to the successful banker——'

'And you needn't use that supercilious tone whenever you mention Richard!' she flashed. 'I've told you, he's worth any amount of you—and he'll know how to make me happy even if we have to live in a back street in Brixton. Not that we will,' she added proudly. 'Richard's one of the most successful men in the City, for his age.'

'Well, isn't that just wonderful,' Jason drawled maddeningly. 'I can see there'll be no need for me to worry about you any further. Richard will look after you from now on, more than adequately.'

'Yes, he will! Certainly better than *you* managed to!' she snapped.

Jason said nothing to that, but she could see the tightened muscles round his jaw that meant he was holding his anger in check. Well, he'd asked for it, she thought mutinously. Maybe from now on he would leave Richard out of their conversations.

She hadn't been following the track with any attention, and paused now to glance around them, realising with a small shock that she had no idea of exactly where they were. True, the track was clear enough, stretching behind them; but the contours of the mountains had changed subtly and she could not have said for certain in which direction home lay. Turn around a couple of times and you'd be lost, she thought, and had a sudden vision of fog descending to obscure the way further. Obviously Jason hadn't been exaggerating the dangers; but she didn't intend to admit as much to him.

'Oh, what's that?' she asked instead, noticing for the first time a small building across a narrow valley. Two or three other tracks led to it, none of them looking particularly well used, but the building itself looked solid enough and almost habitable.

'Come and see.' Jason set off down the hillside, finding a path through the gorse and heather. Linzi followed him, her interest quickened. The building was so far from anywhere; she supposed it must once have been a shepherd's hut.

In fact, as she drew nearer she could see that it had been no such thing. Jumping the narrow stream at the bottom of the valley, she looked up and realised from the shape of its windows that it must be a chapel. As she scrambled up the slope towards it, she wondered why it had been built here and if it were still used.

She wasn't prepared for what met her eyes when Jason swung open the heavy door. And the gasp of pleasure that escaped her lips was purely voluntary and entirely genuine.

'Oh, it's lovely!' She took a step inside. 'May I look around?'

The chapel had evidently been out of use for some time and had been completely cleared inside. It comprised one large room; a room clearly intended for simple though comfortable living. The floor was covered in tough matting which gave a warmth to the interior, the walls white washed. Shelves lined the walls, many of them filled with books; benches and armchairs added to the comfort. At the far end, the floor raised in what had been the chancel, was a large double bed, draped with thick curtains in the style of a fourposter. Close to the door stood a small Calor gas cooker and cupboards to store utensils.

'It's perfect,' Linzi said with delight. 'A real little hideaway. But surely it's not left unlocked?'

Jason shook his head and showed her an iron key. He must have unlocked it while she was still making her way up the slope. Linzi stared at him, a tiny frown drawing her fine brows together.

'Do you mean it's *yours*?' she asked. 'But why? When you've got Bron Melyn?'

Jason shrugged. 'The two came together. I couldn't help having it. Of course, it was never like this when Uncle Walter owned it. It was derelict then—I don't suppose he ever came near the place. Probably hoped it would just quietly fall down. I had to do quite a lot of work to it. But, as you say, it is the perfect hideaway. I often come up here for the odd night or two.'

Oh yes? Linzi thought, remembering suddenly Cindy's hints about Jason's love-life so many years ago. She blushed suddenly, realising what a fool she must have been not to think of it before. Jason wasn't the sort of man to do without women, after all. And what better than a cosy little retreat, tucked away in the hills, for his brief affairs?

Suddenly nervous, she looked up through her lashes at him. Was this why he'd brought her here this afternoon? He had moved close, so that she could feel the heat of his body through her thin T-shirt. She wanted to step away—knew that she ought to step away. But her limbs seemed suddenly powerless to move. Something stronger than her will kept her standing there, breathing in the masculine smell of him, tingling to his nearness. Her breathing quickened and her skin prickled. Almost as if compelled, she raised her face to his, lips softly parted.

'Linzi!' His voice was rough as he took her in his arms. With a feeling of inevitability, she let him mould her against him, felt her softness melt against his hard muscular body. Her eyes closed as his lips took hers; gently at first, tenderly, yet with a hint of restrained passion that shook her and brought a response that had them both gasping. On a groan, his lips hardened, becoming more demanding. Linzi clung to him as his hands moved possessively over her body, roaming from breast to hip with intimate little diversions in between. She felt sure that she would fall; only his strength holding her against him kept her on her feet until she felt him lowering her gently to the floor, laying her on a cushion dragged from the nearest armchair so that he could lean over her and look down into into her face.

'Linzi,' he murmured again, his voice deep now and husky, before his lips once again came down on hers with a gentleness that almost drove her wild. Moving softly, they brushed over hers, exploring, taunting; then crushed down with an urgency she met with equal ardour. All thoughts of the world outside had flown. Richard was a world away as she met Jason's lovemaking with an increasing response that drew a gathering sensuousness from him, and she knew that there could only be one end to this sudden encounter.

Jason had dragged her T-shirt from her jeans to take possession of the breasts that sprang, full and taut, into his hands, and was fumbling with her waistband when Linzi became aware of voices outside. For a moment she turned cold; whoever it was, she couldn't stand them breaking in on this. Suddenly frantic, she wriggled away, pushing at Jason to get his weight off her. His face darkened with frustrated anger; then his head came up and she knew that he too had heard the sounds.

With a muttered oath he dragged her to her feet and they both tidied their clothes, although Linzi didn't have time to tuck in her T-shirt. Shrugging, she left it loose and lifted her hair, shaking it free of tangles. And then the sunlit door was darkened by a shadow as someone peered in. Only the silhouette could be seen, but Linzi stared in fascination as the face looked around the chapel and a tinkling laugh floated through the air.

'So this is where you're hiding yourself! And on this lovely afternoon, too. Why don't you come on out into the sunshine, Jason my love, and introduce me to your new model?'

The voice was pretty, light and musical with a faint Welsh lilt that was very attractive. Linzi had never heard it in her life, but she knew its owner. She had seen that silhouette before. In fact, she had seen the entire head.

A small, neat head, with pretty features, short, curling hair and a flirtatious look about the eyes. A head she had last seen, cast in bronze, in pride of place on a shelf in Jason's studio.

CHAPTER FOUR

SLOWLY, still shaken and trying to control her uneven breathing, Linzi followed Jason out into the sunlight. The sudden dazzle made her blink and it was a moment or two before she was able to see properly; the two figures standing outside the chapel were hazy and blurred. But as her senses cleared, they came into clearer view.

The girl was, as she had thought, the owner of the head she had seen at Bron Melyn. Small and petite, she had the instant effect of making Linzi feel tall and gawky. She had dark hair with a hint of auburn, that curled closely round her well-shaped head, merry dark eyes that flashed from a face as smooth and pale as porcelain, and a small, full-lipped mouth. A very *kissable* mouth, Linzi thought irrelevantly.

With her was a tall, stooping man whom Linzi guessed to be in his sixties. He was looking at her with a kindly interest quite different from his companion's frank curiosity, and Linzi found herself drawn to him at once.

'Well, introduce us, Jason,' the girl exclaimed, and Linzi noticed again the slight, pretty lilt. The shapely body was curved generously, yet still appeared slim enough, and Linzi recognised another of Jason's sculptures in the small hands. She looked at the neat, dark red trouser suit and wondered if Jason considered that a suitable outfit for hill-walking; then curbed her thoughts, telling herself not to be catty. As if it mattered to her what this girl wore, or what Jason thought about it!

Nevertheless, she glanced at him to assess his reaction and found himself, as she had half expected, smiling his devastating smile and looking as pleased as if he were welcoming guests to a party. Only the party was meant for two, she thought, suddenly feeling bereft and let down. Didn't it worry Jason at all that they'd just been interrupted in the most intimate moment they had ever experienced together? Or maybe it wasn't like that for him. Maybe it had been just an opportunity not to be missed; an opportunity that would probably come again anyway. Feeling suddenly cheapened, she moved away, but Jason stopped her.

'Linzi, I'd like you to meet some friends of mine. Thomas Penrhys, who lives at Penrhys Court not far from Bron Melyn; and his daughter Ceri. You've probably noticed bits of Ceri lying about in the studio,' he added with a grin. 'I've done her head several times, and her hands too. One day I'm going to do the whole thing.'

And no doubt you're both looking forward to *that*, Linzi thought sourly. But she smiled at the girl and held out her hand. Was she being especially churlish? There was only friendliness in Ceri's smile, welcome in her handshake. Was it her imagination that something else lurked in the dark, merry eyes? A watchfulness, a shrewd calculation?

'I'm so pleased to meet you,' Ceri exclaimed. 'I've seen your pictures so often. Maybe we can have a good old gossip some time when Jason's not working you too hard. But I'm sure he's not.'

Was there innuendo in that remark? Considering that they had been discovered in the chapel in the middle of the afternoon, there might well be. But perhaps she was being over-sensitive after the emotion of the past hour. Linzi hesitated, but before she could speak old Mr Penrhys came to her rescue.

'Perhaps Jason and Miss Berwick would like to come over to dinner one evening,' he suggested in a mild voice. 'Selwyn will be home soon and we could have a little celebration.'

'Now that *is* a good idea!' Ceri cried. 'Selwyn's my twin brother,' she explained to Linzi. 'He's been in

America, on and off, for the past year. Didn't I hear that you'd just come back from America too? Weren't you in New York?'

'Yes, for quite a while.' Linzi moved uneasily. New York wasn't something she wanted to discuss too much, and if Ceri's brother had been there recently he was almost sure to want to talk about it. But with any luck, it wouldn't be until after she had gone anyway. 'When is your brother coming home?' she asked.

'Oh, we don't know. Selwyn never tells us his movements, he just turns up.' Ceri laughed. 'He's something of an entrepreneur. Something turns up and he's off again. You can't keep track of Selwyn.'

'I live in hopes that the boy will settle down,' Mr Penrhys remarked, 'But there, he's almost thirty now and still doesn't show any signs of it. I've rather given up worrying, I'm afraid.'

'There was never any need to worry about Selwyn anyway,' Ceri told him. 'And how often have I asked you not to tell people his age—don't you realise it gives me away as well!' Her laugh tinkled again. 'Not that it matters with Jason. We've known each other too long and too well to have silly secrets like that from each other, haven't we?'

'We have indeed.' Linzi glanced quickly at him and saw the expression in his eyes as he looked down at Ceri. So she'd been right, she thought dully. Her instincts, that had been screaming at her ever since her first sight of Ceri, telling her that there was more than friendship between her and Jason, were correct. There had to be something between two people who looked at each other the way these two did. Fleetingly, she wondered if it were Ceri that Megan had been referring to. Then she shrugged, turning away from the couple who were now standing close to each other, laughing at some private joke. What did it matter to her anyway? She'd be gone from here and back in London in a few weeks. Ceri was welcome to the black-haired, craggy-faced sculptor. Welcome to his kisses and his lovemaking. . . .

Abruptly, Linzi walked a few quick steps away so that she could no longer hear the quiet laughter. Only a few minutes ago Jason had been kissing *her*—and she had been on the point of surrender. She felt hot as she recalled the whirling sensations of those moments when he had held her in his arms and looked down at her, his face grave and his brilliant eyes dark with desire. How could she have let it happen? When at any other time she hated him, when she wore Richard's engagement ring? What was it about him that had this strange, sensual effect on her?

She had heard that with some people the chemistry between them was powerful enough to be explosive. Presumably that was the way it was with her and Jason. Nothing to do with love or affection. Just a physical reaction; a reaction that could be avoided simply by never allowing it the opportunity to come about. And in future, she determined, that was how she would play this game. Never again would she run the risk of allowing Jason to take advantage of her.

She became aware that Mr Penrhys was speaking to her and she turned quickly, walking beside him down a rough track. Jason and Ceri were following a little way behind, just too far for her to hear what they were saying. Linzi told herself she didn't want to know anyway, and gave her full attention to Mr Penrhys, answering his questions about her life and making him laugh with stories of Paris, Rome and London. Her modelling career had been sufficiently varied for her name and face to be familiar to people from all walks of life; she wasn't surprised when Mr Penrhys mentioned one or two TV adverts she had been successful in.

'But you're giving it up now, aren't you?' Ceri asked in her light voice, catching them up. 'Aren't you getting married—to some high-finance whizz-kid, or someone like that?'

'Yes, more or less.' Linzi smiled at the thought of Richard being called a whizz-kid, yet that was what he was really, she supposed. 'Richard's away in Europe at present, but he'll be back soon and then we'll be busy arranging the wedding and deciding where to live. So I shan't have time for modelling after this.'

'Jason's lucky you were still available, then,' Ceri murmured, slanting a provocative look up at him from under her thick dark lashes. 'Of course, I offered to model for him, but he seems to have some special idea in mind that I wouldn't be right for. . . .'

'Now, we've been through all that before, Ceri,' Jason told her, his smile robbing the words of any rebuke. 'You know that you're special—I've done enough models of you for you to realise that—but for this particular commission Linzi is the type I need.' And that puts me in my place, Linzi thought. Not special—just a type. She turned back to Ceri's father.

'This is the first time I've really been up here,' she remarked, waving an expressive hand at the surrounding hills. 'It's so beautiful I never want to go down. Have you lived here all your life, Mr Penrhys?'

'Oh yes. We're an old local family, you know. Of course, we don't own all the land we used to—just the Court and a few fields and one or two of the hills now. A lot of it was sold off just before I inherited. All we old families are poor as church mice now, you know!'

'Bron Melyn used to belong to us,' Ceri put in. 'Or didn't Jason tell you that?'

'No—we haven't had much time for talking.' But that wasn't quite true. There'd been many times, at meals or late in the evenings when they'd been listening to music together, when such an item of information might have fallen quite naturally into the conversation. Perhaps Jason hadn't thought she'd be interested. Hadn't realised that she was falling in love with Bron Melyn, that anything to do with the sturdy old farmhouse and its dramatic backcloth of hills was likely to catch at her imagination.

When they reached the end of the track, Linzi found that the lane it led to went directly past Penrhys Court. Mr Penrhys and Ceri left them there, but Ceri agreed delightedly to Jason's suggestion that she come over to Bron Melyn for dinner that evening.

'It seems ages since we had an evening together,' she said reproachfully. 'Not since the dinner we had together in Chepstow. Almost a fortnight ago!'

'Well, we'll make up for it tonight,' Jason told her, smiling. 'And you and Linzi can have that gossip you were wanting.'

The two girls glanced at each other. Ceri's expression was difficult to read—but Linzi was sure her smile went no deeper than the surface. She didn't want an evening spent in girl-talk, that was plain. What Ceri wanted was an evening with Jason—full stop.

Hugh had tea ready when they returned to Bron Melyn and Linzi, thirsty after the long hot walk, drank several cups. Afterwards, she went up to her room and read for a while. It was quiet and peaceful up there, with no sound but a faint tapping coming from the studio, where Jason had gone, and the faraway bleating of sheep on the hill.

After a while she began to prepare for dinner, washing her hair and taking a long, leisurely shower. Usually she and Jason dressed informally, he casual in pale slacks and a shirt that showed off his broad, muscular shoulders and narrow waist, she in a loose caftan or summer dress. But tonight she felt that something more was called for. She stared into her wardrobe for a long time before finally deciding on a long dress of sea-green silk chiffon in Grecian style, with a low scooped neckline and slashed, elbow-length sleeves that accentuated the slimness of her arms. With it she wore silver chains looped around her long neck, and silver sandals. Her tawny hair she swept up into a French pleat, and from her ears she hung long silver ear-rings.

Her heartbeat quickened as she looked into the mirror and knew that she had never looked lovelier. Normally she took her looks very much for granted; now she saw them through another's eyes, and she wondered what Jason's reaction might be. So far, he had seen her only in casual clothes. But with Ceri there to make her look tall and ungainly, would he even notice that his little 'sister' had grown up?

Linzi frowned as she thought of their walk home after leaving Penrhys Court. Jason had been silent, deep in thought. And Linzi, acutely aware of the tension between them, the memory of his kisses in the chapel still burning her mind, had been unable to think of a word to say. It was only as they came in sight of Bron Melyn that he had stopped abruptly and spoken.

'Linzi, don't go in yet. There's something I want to say to you.'

'Oh?' Linzi paused, her nerves tingling. What could he possibly want to say? That he was sorry for what had happened in the chapel, that he hadn't meant it? That there was nothing between him and Ceri? She wouldn't believe either of them. To her, Jason Carver had proved himself to be nothing but an opportunist. Carrying on an affair with one girl while ready at any moment to start another with someone else. Or would it have been a once-only occasion? Whatever the answer, she didn't want to know. More than that, she didn't want Jason to know the way it had affected her.

'Linzi, wait. We need to talk——'

'You may, I don't,' she said tightly. 'All right, I enjoyed it too—but it didn't mean anything, did it? You don't have to explain or apologise. I've been around, you know. I didn't waste those five years. I don't expect men to have honourable intentions.'

Jason stared at her, his face darkening. It was quite plain what construction he had put on her words—well, let him, Linzi thought, shrugging. Maybe it was better that way. If he thought she was experienced, he would think she could control her own reactions. Wouldn't run away with the idea that a kiss or a touch from him would have her weak at the knees, as malleable in his hands as the clay he used to model.

If only he knew!

Keeping up a defiant pretence, Linzi watched him. So now he believed that the moments in the chapel were just pleasurable dalliance. Good! And if she could further convince him that she wasn't interested in repeating the experiment, that should keep her safe. After all, he had Ceri—all too willing a partner, she'd guess—to turn to, to relieve any frustration he might experience. And, no doubt, there were others too. . . .

'So I don't need to apologise,' Jason said slowly.

'Indeed not. At least, not for the fact that you tried.' Linzi picked a bracken frond from the bank and plucked at it. 'But don't bother again. As I say, it was quite enjoyable, but . . .' She shrugged, leaving him to complete the sentence.

Which he evidently did. 'Not up to Richard's standard, I guess,' he said with heavy irony, and Linzi felt her fists clench as the familiar indignation rose within her. Somehow she kept her voice level as she faced him.

'No! Nowhere near, if you must know. And I've told you before, keep that tone out of your voice when you mention Richard—or don't mention him at all! He's out of your league, Jason Carver—way, way out of your league!'

Summoning all her reserves, she held Jason's stare. The thought of the afternoon's kisses almost weakened her with the knowledge that nothing she had said was true—but she dared not let Jason see it. Once he knew his effect on her, she would have no defence. Richard was her only safeguard against him.

Jason's eyes were a cold blue as he looked back at her, and she knew a sudden qualm. She must now have lost for ever any good opinion he might have had of her. And suddenly, unable to tolerate his gaze any longer, she

turned away and walked through the gate and into the
yard. For once, the sight of the house gave her no pleasure
at all. She scarcely acknowledged Hugh's welcoming smile
as she walked slowly through to the terrace and sank down
on one of the chairs.

Jason didn't reappear, and Linzi was left to drink her
tea in peace and to reflect on the way she felt compelled
to leap to Richard's defence whenever Jason mentioned
his name. Even to the extent of exaggerating his abilities,
she admitted ruefully. Because she knew that Richard had
never roused her to one-tenth of the passion that Jason
had. And probably never would.

Well, all right. Wasn't that what she wanted?

Thinking this over, Linzi wondered why she was now
concerned to make an impression at dinner tonight. Was
it just ordinary female competitiveness, or something
more? Professional pride, perhaps—Ceri would certainly
be expecting the famous model to appear as something
special and would no doubt make an effort of her own.
Or was there some deeper instinct involved?

Shrugging her slim shoulders, she turned to the door
and opened it. The sun had set and dusk pervaded the
passage and stairs. Linzi switched on the light and began
to go down.

'Yes,' said Jason's voice from below, 'you make a very
effective model.'

Linzi paused, staring at him as he came out of the
shadows. Her pulses quickened. It was the first time she
had seen him in formal clothes, and the dinner-jacket and
dazzling white shirt suited his dark, saturnine good looks.
His eyes were like sapphires as he watched her, and from the
cuffs of his shirt the colour was picked up by jewelled links.

Linzi came down slowly, still transfixed. This was a
different Jason from the one she knew. But did she know
him at all? There were so many unsuspected sides to
him—she was beginning to wonder.

'That dress,' said Jason, walking round her as she

reached the hall, 'is what you must wear for the figure. It's exactly what I had in mind and it suits you to perfection.' He looked into her eyes and as she saw his face change something seemed to move inside her. 'Linzi, I've got to talk to you. I wish to hell——' But what he wished, she didn't find out; for at that moment the doorbell rang.

Ceri was, as Linzi had expected, dressed in a way that exactly suited her petite beauty, and in a way directly designed to appeal to men. Her dress was ruby-red, setting off her dark hair and eyes and accentuating her pale complexion. The plunging neckline did little to conceal the full, ripe breasts, reaching almost to the tiny waist below which the skirt billowed. One day, Linzi thought, Ceri would have a weight problem. Just now, looking at the curvaceous figure and provocative eyes and mouth, she couldn't blame any man for wanting to take her straight to bed.

The meal was a good one, cooked exquisitely by Hugh, who joined them for it. It was clear that he and Jason were good friends rather than employer and man, and Linzi had already realised just how invaluable Hugh was, both as cook and 'general dogsbody', as he had described himself, and as secretary. She ate the smoked mackerel pâté that formed the first course with relish, and asked Hugh if he had made it himself.

'Oh yes. I've always enjoyed cooking. But don't fill yourself up with it, Linzi—' she'd asked him to call her that on her second day '—I've something special for the main course.'

'Hugh!' Ceri clasped her hands. 'You haven't made my favourite?'

'If your favourite happens to be boeuf bourguignon, yes,' Hugh answered, and his eyes met Linzi's in a flash of amusement. She had the sudden idea that whatever he had prepared would have proved to be Ceri's favourite, and smiled, wondering how Jason could be taken in by such an obvious approach. Clearly, Hugh wasn't.

The casserole arrived, accompanied by jacket potatoes and salad, and Linzi tasted it with enthusiasm. But her enjoyment was marred by the way Ceri had moved her chair a fraction nearer to Jason's, so that their arms touched; by the way she kept all the conversation and attention directed upon herself, with tiny, flirtatious movements and glances; and by the way that Linzi herself was gradually excluded, so that the party eventually became a tête-à-tête between Jason and Ceri, with Hugh and herself as mere onlookers.

It was with relief that, when the hazelnut meringue had been finished and Hugh had gone to the kitchen to fetch the coffee, she heard the phone ring and realised that it was probably Richard. She hurried out to the hall to speak to him.

'Yes, yes, I'm fine,' she said when they were finally connected. 'It's lovely to hear you. Yes, everything's all right.' Quickly she gave him the outline of her assignment, adding that she'd known Jason for years, he had lived as one of her family. 'Where are you going next? Are there any changes in your schedule?'

'Only one so far. The hotel's been changed in Vienna— a fire or something. Wait a moment, I'll read out the address.' Linzi wrote it down, repeating it to make sure she got it right. 'Now, you will keep in touch, won't you, darling? Letters ought to reach me now, if you don't want to use the phone. I'll ring you when I can, will that be all right?'

'Yes. Yes, please ring, Richard.' Linzi held the phone close against her ear, suddenly longing for his reassuring presence. 'Goodbye, darling. I'll write soon. 'Bye. . . .'

The phone went dead and she held it for a moment before replacing it. Richard had sounded so very far away. She wished that he'd never had to go, feeling uneasily that nothing could ever be quite the same again. This parting was going to change things between them, and she didn't want it to. Then she shook herself angrily. She was letting herself get fanciful! Letting Richard's fears get through to her, even though he had seemed reassured tonight. . . . Abruptly, she put back the receiver and turned to go into the sitting-room.

Ceri was there alone. She looked up and smiled as Linzi came in.

'I take it that was your fiancé. Is everything going well?'

'Yes, fine.' Linzi dropped on to the sofa. 'He's going on to Vienna soon. Keeping abreast of our banking connections in other capitals.' She paused. 'You know, I feel sure I've seen you before—and not just in bronze in Jason's studio.'

Ceri smiled. 'I'm an actress. Oh, not terribly serious— but I've done a bit of TV. That may be where you've seen me. I'm not working at the moment.' She gave her tinkling laugh. 'The trouble is, I was a stage-struck teenager, and happened to have some talent as well. But I don't think the stage is for me really—I'm too lazy. By the time I'd discovered what hard work it all is, I'd become established, in a small way, and now I don't know what else I could do.' Her glance this time was pure mischief. 'Marry a rich man, I suppose is the answer—but he'd have to be local. I couldn't leave Wales.'

The implication was obvious, as obvious as the 'keep off the grass' flash of the eyes that accompanied it. Linzi raised her eyebrows. She had no intention of trespassing in that particular meadow, and she would have liked to tell Ceri so—but something stopped her. Let the other girl think what she liked! There was no official understanding between her and Jason, and until there was she would have to take her chance. There was no need, no need at all, to let her know that Linzi was no competition. If an engagement ring wasn't enough to tell her that, then nothing else would convince her anyway.

Maybe Ceri was ruthless enough herself to take another girl's fiancé if she wanted him. And believed that every other girl was the same. In which case, she deserved to worry a little.

The door, left ajar, pushed open as Bracken came
through ahead of Jason, who was carrying a tray of
coffee. The two girls watched as he set it down, explaining that Hugh had decided to deal with some correspond-
ence, and Linzi took the cup he handed to her, refusing
sugar.

'You never remember that,' she remarked lightly. 'I've
never taken sugar, even as a child.'

'A child?' Ceri pounced. 'How long have you known
Jason, then?'

'Oh, always.' Linzi smiled. 'My parents brought him
up. Haven't you told her that, Jason? He was practically
my brother.'

'*Your* parents?' Ceri looked put out. 'Well, I knew about
his early life, of course—but I never connected it with
you——'

'No reason why you should, since I never told you that.'
Jason lounged easily across to draw the curtains. 'And I'd
be obliged if the two of you would refrain from discussing
me as if I weren't here! Look——' he glanced at his
watch '——there are one or two of those letters that I need
to deal with myself. D'you mind if I leave you for half an
hour? And you can spend the time discussing me to your
hearts' content!'

His grin was wicked, turning Linzi's heart over even
though she knew that it was at Ceri it was mostly directed.
He picked up his coffee-cup and drained it; then left the
room with an easy stride, followed by the big Alsatian and
leaving the two girls in an uncomfortable silence.

'So you and Jason were brought up together,' Ceri said
at last. 'That must have been—interesting.'

'Oh, yes. Though of course by the time I was old
enough to take notice, he was away a good deal. I suppose
that's why I looked up to him so much. Hero-worshipped
him, if you like. I just lived for the times when he came
home.'

'I see.' Ceri stirred her coffee, the soft lamplight glowing

on her ruby-red dress and gleaming dark curls. 'And now?
Is he still your—hero?'

Linzi laughed. 'Oh, I hardly think so! We haven't even
met for five years.' No need to mention the disastrous
engagement; that was a memory still too tender to explore.

'And now you're together again. Didn't you think it
seemed strange—Jason thinking of you after all that
time?'

'Not really. It's purely professional.' But it was clear
that Ceri didn't believe this, and Linzi made no attempt
to emphasise it. 'Of course, when you're really close to
someone time doesn't seem all that important. . . .'

Ceri's head snapped up. 'But you're engaged to
someone else, aren't you? You're not interested in Jason—
you can't be.' She paused as if considering, then added in
a voice full of venom, 'Look, let's stop beating about the
bush. I'm quite well aware of what was going on in that
chapel this afternoon. Dad and I came along just in time,
didn't we? You thought you'd have Jason nicely snared—
and it didn't work. And it *won't* work, either. All right,
he's susceptible—what man isn't when a girl with your
kind of looks throw herself at his head? Not Jason,
anyway—he's always been ready to take his opportunities,
and why not? But it wouldn't have meant anything even
if I hadn't come along. Because *I* mean to have Jason
Carver. I've been working towards it for years—ever since
he first came here. He's not been an easy fish to play, but
I'm just on the edge of hooking him now, and I'm not
having all that time and patience wasted. So just you take
yourself back to London, Linzi Berwick, and marry your
banker. Whatever idea it is you've got in your head, it
isn't going to work—I'll make damned sure of that!'

Linzi gazed at her, appalled by the change in the pretty
Welsh features, now distorted by jealousy and rage.
Guiltily, she realised that this outburst was at least partly
her own fault; she'd led Ceri along, allowed her to believe

that there could be something between her and Jason.
Yet had that made so very much difference? Ceri had
made up her mind about her the moment they'd met.
Nothing Linzi could have said or done would have altered
that. Or—she blushed at the thought—altered the fact
that Ceri was quite right about what had happened in
the chapel.

'Look,' she said, 'I don't know what you're getting so
upset about, but there's really no need. Jason and I have
been all through that scene, years ago. It didn't work
then and it wouldn't work now, even if we both wanted it
to—and I can assure you neither of us does. What
happened in the chapel this afternoon was just as you
say—opportunity. And it's not going to happen again.
I've got my own life to lead and I don't need complica-
tions like Jason Carver in it.'

Ceri's eyes narrowed. Whether she believed her or not,
Linzi couldn't tell, and the way she was feeling now she
didn't really care.

'All right, then,' the Welsh girl said, her voice silky. 'So
you won't mind going back to London, will you?
Straightaway.'

Linzi stared at her. 'Of course I can't! There's the
figure—Jason needs——'

'Jason doesn't need you! Look, until a couple of weeks
ago I was going to be the model for that figure, or didn't
you know that? It was going to be a great thing for me—
it would have helped my career and I'd have had all the
time in the world to work on Jason too. And then he got
this other idea and nothing would do but he had to have
you. How do you think I felt about that? And then you
arrive and Jason's too busy to see me or anyone else, yet
he seems to have plenty of time to take you for walks in
the hills——'

'That was the first time!' Linzi interrupted. 'And it
wasn't arranged, I'd set out on my own.'

'So he followed you.' Ceri's eyes flashed with temper

and her full bosom heaved. 'And don't say you haven't been encouraging him—I've seen the way you've been looking at him tonight. And at me—if looks could kill I'd have vanished in a puff of smoke.'

'You're imagining it——'

'Oh, no, I'm not! I don't know who you're trying to convince, Linzi Berwick, maybe it's yourself, but it certainly isn't me. I can recognise that look in another girl's eyes. You've got your rich banker—but you're still going to make a play for the successful sculptor. Well, I'll tell you this—it's not going to work. I'll do everything I can to make sure of that. You might just as well do as I suggested, Miss Berwick—go straight back to London. Because if you stay here, you're going to find things getting very, very uncomfortable.'

'Oh, don't be so ridiculous!' Linzi snapped, her patience at an end. 'I'm not making a play for Jason, and I'm certainly not going back to London. Not until the job's finished, anyway. And I really don't see what you think you can do about that!'

'No?' Ceri stood up and picked up her velvet evening bag. 'Well, we'll have to see, won't we? I don't think I'll wait for Jason to come back. You can tell him I had to go—see if you can explain that away, for a start.' She paused, looking down at Linzi, and her pretty, sweet face was twisted with spite. 'You'll be sorry, you know. I'm not just a little local girl, after all—I've got contacts. And I shan't hesitate to use them!'

Linzi turned away, too sickened to answer. How could Jason be taken in by this pretty little virago? But then he had probably never seen this side of Ceri, she mused as the other girl slammed out of the room. He would have seen only her sweetness and gaiety. And she hoped fervently that Ceri never would get her way. Even Jason Carver didn't deserve that!

The door opened and Jason came in, looking round in surprise to find her alone.

'What's happened?' he asked. 'Has Ceri gone? I thought I heard a car—didn't she realise I was coming back?'

'Oh, she realised,' Linzi said dully. 'She just—got tired of the company, I think.'

He stared at her his eyes narrowing. 'What do you mean by that? What happened between you two?' With a single stride he was beside her, his hands on her arms. 'Tell me, damn you—what have you been saying to her?'

'Nothing!' Linzi twisted violently, but his fingers only tightened on her. 'Jason, let me go!'

'*Nothing?*' The lines on his face deepened in disbelief. 'Don't give me that! Ceri would never have gone off like that if she hadn't been provoked—and provoked beyond tolerance. She's one of the sweetest-natured girls I know, and if you've hurt her——'

'*I* hurt *her?*' Linzi gasped. 'Jason, you don't know what you're saying. Your sweet, charming Ceri can more than look after herself, believe me. She knows exactly what she wants and she goes all out to get it. You never told me she wanted to model for you for this figure.'

'There was no need! It was never a serious proposition. Oh, I considered it, yes—but Ceri just wasn't right for what I had in mind. She understood that.' He dropped his hands and his eyes searched hers. 'Linzi, if you're out to make trouble, I warn you it's not going to work. What is it with you anyway? Jealousy?' His anger was growing as he spoke and Linzi stared up at him, frightened by the menace in his eyes. 'My God, Linzi, you just about take the biscuit. I can see now I was wrong about you all those years ago. I thought you'd get over your flightiness once you'd got a man of your own—thought you'd be happy enough then to let other girls have a chance. But you haven't changed, have you? You still want everything in trousers. You've got your man, you've got your nice expensive meal-ticket all lined up, but even that isn't good enough for you.' His hands came down to her arms and jerked her roughly to her feet. 'Let him get a nice safe distance across the Channel and off you go again. Oh, don't think I haven't seen you giving Hugh the eye—even young Alun isn't beneath you, is he? And as for me—well, I thank God on my knees that Ceri and her father came along when they did this afternoon, or there's no knowing what might have happened. And to think I read some genuine feeling into your response!'

'Jason, it's not like that!' He was holding her close, his breath quick and warm on her cheeks, and she felt the thunder of her heart increasing intolerably. 'Let me go! Jason, please!'

'Let you go?' he muttered thickly. 'Why in hell should I? Don't you deserve to be taught a lesson? Don't you realise you've been driving me wild ever since the first moment you stepped through that door? And all these years when I've had only photographs to go by? Let you go? You have to be joking! I tried to hold back, telling myself you were engaged to another man, kidding myself you were a virgin still—but I was wrong, wasn't I? You've been playing the field for years—giving other men what you wouldn't give me.' His powerful arms lifted her easily, swinging her through the door, and as he mounted the stairs his voice went on, low and husky, distorted by anger and desire. 'So you've been around,' he mocked, throwing back at her the words she'd flung at him that afternoon. 'You don't expect men to have honourable intentions.' He kicked open the door to her bedroom. 'You won't expect me to have them then, will you!'

'Jason!' she gasped, thoroughly frightened now. 'Jason, listen—Jason, I beg you, don't——' But her words stopped abruptly as Jason flung her on to the bed and crushed his whole weight down on her. His lips found hers, cruelly demanding, with none of the tenderness she had experienced before, forcing her mouth open, his teeth bruising her lips. Frantically, she wriggled under his body, but her movements only seemed to incite him further and he groaned as his hands gripped her waist and moved up over her breasts. Fumblingly, he raised her from the bed and felt for the long back zip, dragging it down so that he could pull the soft material down to her waist. The bra seemed to disappear almost of its own volition, and as he stared at the fullness of her breasts and then buried his face in them, Linzi knew that she had no more strength to protest. The chemistry was working again, whether or not she wanted it to; and she whimpered softly as she let her own arms slide round his body and ran her fingers through the black, silver-dusted hair.

'Jason,' she whispered. 'Jason—oh, Jason. . . .'

The harshness had gone from his lips and his hands. Tenderly they moved over her, caressing, exploring, bringing to her soaring heart a delight that was greater than any yet. Beneath their expertise she felt herself grow limp, her movements languorous, her body stiffening only a little when his fingers ventured more intimately, until at last Jason raised himself and stared down at her, his eyes almost black and his brows contracting.

'Linzi,' he murmured. 'Linzi, what's happening to us? I brought you up here meaning to give you the lesson of your life, and instead—I've never known anything like it. What's going on?' He watched her as she moved under him, barely conscious of anything but the pulsing demands of her body. 'You look—scared. Are you, *cariad*? Are you frightened of me? You've no need to be, I swear it.'

Linzi let her tawny eyes, darkened now to a velvet brown, meet his. At this moment she knew that he could if he chose read the truth, the truth that was in her heart and that until now she had not admitted even to herself. And that other truth—the truth that she had to tell him.

'Yes,' she whispered, 'I am frightened—just a little. You see—this is my first time. I—I let you think there'd been others, but it's not true. I—I've never slept with a man before, Jason.'

For a long moment he held her eyes, his own widening

with shock. He let his glance move down her body—past the slender neck, over the smooth shoulders, lingering on the full rounded breasts. Then, very gently, he drew the soft green material up to cover her. He bent and kissed her bemused eyes with a softness that was the complete opposite from his harsh treatment of her only a few minutes earlier, then he stood up from the bed.

Linzi blinked up at him, bewildered, but he smiled as he shook his head at her.

'You ought to be more careful what you tell people,' he said softly. 'You nearly had yourself some real trouble there. . . . Linzi, we're going to have to talk this out, but first we both need time to think. Look, I have to go away tomorrow—only down to Newport about the foundry work, but it means staying overnight. It'll do us good to be apart for a while, get ourselves sorted out—but when I come back, we'll have that talk, all right?' His finger traced a pattern on her cheek. 'You won't go running away in the meantime?'

'I won't run away,' Linzi promised in a whisper, and he nodded.

'I'll leave you now, then.' For a moment he hesitated, his eyes dark with longing. 'I want to kiss you again, Linzi,' he muttered, 'but I don't think I trust myself—oh, what the hell. . . .' And she clung to him as his black hair fell across her face and his lips sought hers. Her blood leapt; she wanted to keep him with her, tell him it didn't matter that she was a virgin, that she'd been waiting for just this moment—but almost before she had time to think, he had wrenched himself out of her arms and was a yard away, his hand on the door. He ran a trembling hand through the wild hair, closed his eyes deliberately to shut her out—and was gone.

And although Linzi lay awake for most of the night, acutely aware that he was only yards away down the passage, he did not come back.

CHAPTER FIVE

JASON had left by the time Linzi got up next morning. He had set off early, Hugh told her, in the hope that he might be able to get through his discussions by that evening and come straight home. Linzi nodded. She would go down to Crickhowell, she decided, and get the clothes that Jason had told her were necessary for walking in the mountains—waterproofs, a small rucksack to carry them in, and a pair of boots. Then she would be ready to take Bracken for his walk this afternoon.

'That's a good idea,' Hugh approved. 'You'll be all right with Bracken. Keep to the tracks, though. That dog can go for miles and he may think you're just as keen!'

Linzi laughed and promised to be careful. She stretched lazily, gazing up the valley as she drank her coffee. It was rather nice to have a day's holiday—although, rather to her surprise, she found herself missing Jason and wondering already just when he would get back.

She had slept only fitfully last night, waking several times convinced that she could feel Jason's arms around her, his kisses on her lips. She still felt bemused by the change in his attitude. He had been so furious with her—so angry on Ceri's behalf. After the quarrel with the Welsh girl, Linzi had been shaken and upset, but Jason hadn't even noticed—had blamed her outright, without even wondering what the truth might be, convinced at the outset that the trouble must have been caused by Linzi. And then it had seemed that his control had snapped, all the frustration of years had been unleashed and that nothing could have saved her from the inevitable outcome. At that moment, as Jason carried her up the stairs and flung her roughly on to her bed, Linzi had felt a

82

terror she had never before experienced. Oh, she had wanted Jason, she had to admit that—as up there in the chapel she had wanted him with an urgency that had transcended anything she had ever felt before. For, in spite of her vows never to get deeply involved with any man, Linzi had had her share of admirers, and her share of kisses too. Plenty of men had wanted to go further— but desire had never taken hold of Linzi as it had when she was in Jason's arms.

Her fear of Jason last night had been because of the way in which he was about to take her. His own furious anger and determination to teach her a lesson, coupled with his belief that she was already experienced, had led him to handle her with a violence he hadn't shown before. And Linzi had known that if ever she and Jason were to come together, it mustn't be this way. Between them sex had to be more than just a physical encounter. It had to be the expression of love.

Love. It was the first time Linzi had allowed that word to enter her thoughts of Jason. She sat quite still, letting the idea float through her mind. *Did* she love Jason? There had been a time, years ago, when she had thought she did. But that had been mere puppy-love, she could see that now. She had been right not to trust it, right to retreat from marriage.

And now? Was it really love that she felt, this singing of the blood whenever Jason was near, this instant response to his touch? Was it love that set her trembling when he let his sapphire eyes move over her in appreciation of her body, or search her own with that strange, compelling question in their brilliant depths? Was it love that weakened all her resolves when she was in his arms, so that the whole world faded and all that mattered was Jason, his hardness and throbbing desire and the longing that rose within her to match his own? Or was it, as she had told herself yesterday, merely chemistry? Merely a desire for physical satisfaction, a brief fulfilment, an assuagement of a biological need.

And if that were so, would she have had this feeling that love should—must—accompany any experience they shared? Wouldn't she just have gone ahead and enjoyed what Jason had to give?

There was no escaping the answer. Reluctantly, she had to admit it—she had fallen in love with Jason Carver. Some time during the past few days—some time as they shared their meals or sat listening to the music they both loved, or perhaps as they worked together in the studio— she had, without even realising it, grown to love him. And now it was too late to retract. Her feelings were ir- revocable.

Restlessly, Linzi got up from the table and walked to the end of the terrace, laying her hand on the great slab of marble that stood there. The surface was smooth, polished; smoothed and polished by the same hands that had caressed her last night, the same fingers that had held her so cruelly before they had relaxed into tenderness.

Linzi thought again of that tenderness, so unexpected after the violent anger Jason had shown only moments before. What had changed him? Why had his harshness melted, his movements ceased to be deliberately painful and become gentle instead? Was it because he too was aware of the chemistry between them, the reaction of skin against skin that brought delight in place of anger, sweetness instead of bitterness? Was there a chance—even a faint one—that love might be growing in him too?

His words had seemed to imply that there could be. But Linzi hardly dared hope that they might. Couldn't they also mean that he could no longer take the risk of keeping her in his house? With an engagement of his own in the offing—and Linzi remembered with a stab the looks that had passed between him and Ceri—he could hardly want to take the risk of upsetting things. He had already accused her of hurting Ceri, never dreaming that it might be the other way about. It was quite possible that he meant to terminate her contract when he returned—send her back to London, unwanted, and forget all about her.

Linzi let her head droop so that her forehead rested against the cool marble. Her thoughts were too confused now to make any sense at all. She just didn't know what might be in Jason's mind. All she knew was that he was firmly ensconced in her heart—always had been, perhaps. Maybe she had been loving him, deep down, all these years. And that was why she had sworn never to marry. Why she had never let any man come near her; why she had never before known the shattering effect of desire.

She was awakened from her thoughts by Hugh, who appeared through the patio door to tell her that there was a telephone call for her.

'A phone call?' Her heart leapt. 'Is it Jason?'

'No.' Hugh looked curiously at her. 'It's from Vienna.'

'Vienna!' It must be Richard. He must have travelled overnight to have reached there so quickly. She hurried indoors and through to the hall, picking up the receiver with trembling fingers.

'Richard? Is that you? Is everything all right?'

'Yes, of course.' He sounded impatient. 'Linzi, there's something I want to say to you. . . . Are you listening?'

'Yes.' Bewilderment showed in her voice; what could Richard have to say so urgently? 'But——'

'Just listen. I want you to go back to London—leave Wales. You've been there over a week, haven't you? Carver can manage without you now, I'm sure.'

'No, he can't, he's only just begun modelling. Richard, I can't leave now——'

'You've got to.' His tone was peremptory. 'I don't want any arguments about this, Linzi. Just get packed now and leave. You can be back in London by this evening.'

'But I *can't* do that!' Linzi was irritated by his assumption that he could order her about. 'I've signed a contract. Anyway, I wouldn't want to run out halfway through the job. It's important to Jason——'

'That doesn't matter.'

'It *does* matter. And it's important to me, too.' She took a deep breath. 'Richard, if you want me to leave you've got to give me some reason. I can't just pack up and go without some idea why. You seemed quite happy about things last night when I spoke to you. What's made you change your mind?'

'Linzi, I don't want to spend a lot of time and money arguing. But if you won't just do as I ask—and I hope you're not going to behave like this after we're married—then I'll tell you this. I was talking to a man on the plane from Hamburg last night—a man who knows Carver. Apparently the fellow's a rake, a womaniser, totally untrustworthy. The man I spoke to said he wouldn't let his fiancée get within a mile of him. *Now* do you understand?'

Linzi was silent. Her heart sank as she listened to Richard's words, and again her seesawing emotions took another dive. Jason a womaniser, a rake? Could it be true? She thought of his behaviour with her—in the chapel, in her own bedroom last night—and his obvious friendship with Ceri, and knew that it could. And yet if that were so, would he have behaved as he did last night? Would he have listened to her assertion of virginity, covered her up and left her?

'Yes, I understand how you feel, Richard,' she said at last. 'But you don't have to believe that. Who was this man anyway? A complete stranger! Why do you take his word for it? I told you, I've known Jason all my life, I——'

'And that's another thing,' he broke in. 'Why was there all this secrecy? If you've known him so well, why couldn't he say who he was? I thought at the time there was something fishy, and now I'm even more sure. I want you away from there, Linzi. You're to pack your things and go back to London, and I don't want any more arguing!'

Anger seethed inside Linzi as she listened to these words. She felt her fingers tighten on the receiver and knew that her voice was rising as she retorted:

'Oh, so you don't! Well, I'm afraid *I* do—I'm not just packing up and leaving like that, just because you've been listening to some scurrilous gossip on the plane from a man you've never even set eyes on before. And you needn't shout at me like that, Richard—I can hear you perfectly well.'

'Linzi, I'm *telling* you——' he began, and at that Linzi let herself go.

'*Telling* me?' she blazed. '*Telling* me? And just what gives you the right to tell me *anything*, Richard? What gives you the right to order me about? We may be engaged, but we're not married yet, you know, and until we are I run my own life, make no mistake about it! And I shall be thinking very seriously about whether we *do* get married, at this rate. I knew you were stuffy and old-fashioned, but I didn't think your ideas went right back to Queen Victoria—I didn't think you intended to be a tyrant!'

'*Tyrant?*' Richard squeaked at the other end of the phone. 'Stuffy? Linzi, have you lost all reason? My God, what's been happening to you down there? Look, for the last time, are you or are you not going back to London?'

'Not!' Linzi yelled back. 'Not, not, *not!*' And without waiting for Richard's reply, she banged down the receiver and stood glowering at it, breathing fast and aware of a strange exhilaration coursing through her veins.

'That's the way to tell 'em,' a voice remarked from the kitchen door. 'Tell them where to get off. It's the only way to keep your end up.'

Linzi turned, startled, and saw Megan standing there, wrapped in her overall and clutching a broom and dust-pan as if she were Britannia. For a second or two Linzi was completely at a loss. Then she began to laugh—and, for the first time for weeks, felt truly lighthearted.

'I'm just going into Crickhowell,' she told the plump little Welshwoman. 'I've got some important shopping to do!'

Well, Linzi thought, she had certainly committed herself now. She stood outside the shop in Crickhowell, her purchases clutched in her arms—a scarlet rucksack, blue waterproof anorak and trousers, and a pair of sturdy leather boots with deep treads on the soles.

'And you'll be needing some thick socks to go with them,' the man in the shop had advised her. 'Two pairs will be most comfortable. You ought to try the boots on with them before you buy, you'll probably need a larger size.'

'I certainly shall, with those on my feet!' Linzi had looked at her feet with amusement, wondering what Anna would say if she could see her now. And Richard! He would be horrified—the only time they'd been for a walk together had been in Windsor one weekend, and he had worried the whole time about the damp grass staining his best suede shoes.

She crossed the square to her Mini and stowed the parcels inside. Now for a cup of coffee, and then she'd be ready to head back to Bron Melyn. Already she was looking forward to her walk that afternoon. And, by buying her waterproofs and boots, she felt that she'd made some kind of declaration. A pledge to Bron Melyn, a promise that she was staying. Whatever protest Richard made.

A small frown creased her brow as she went into a small cafe near the edge of the square. She had surprised herself with her reaction to Richard's suggestion—or order—that she should leave Bron Melyn immediately. She had been on the point of coming to that very decision herself, just before Hugh had called her to the phone. Her own love for Jason admitted and acknowledged, she was too uncertain of his feelings to have any hopes in that direction. She'd even wondered if he might be going to send her away anyway. So why had Richard's call made such a difference? Was her reaction pure defiance—or was it something more?

Linzi sipped her coffee and acknowledged the fact that she would have to think very carefully indeed about her relationship with Richard. His behaviour towards her over the phone had shaken her deeply; up till now he had always seemed quiet and amenable, more than ready to agree to whatever she suggested, ever eager to please. She had seen their future together as being without difficulties—a smooth and easy path, their relationship more that of close companions than lovers. A home, family—a rather vague and indeterminate family of well-ordered children probably spending a good deal of their time at boarding schools—and a pleasant social life; those were the things Linzi had visualised. And Richard himself would be away most of the time too, either working long hours in the City or abroad on business trips, on which she might herself accompany him.

With a shock, Linzi realised that her ideas about the future had been both vague and impossibly rosy. Had she really expected that Richard would be so compliant? That she would be able to lead what amounted to her own life on his money? She felt herself flush as the implications struck home. Jason had referred to Richard as her 'meal-ticket'. Had he been so very far from the truth?

But I love Richard, she told herself, and experienced a second shock as she wondered if that were really true. *Did* she love him? Did she, for instance, react to him in the way that she did to Jason?

Linzi groaned and set down her cup. It was all too complicated. What she needed was a good walk on the hills, with Bracken bounding along beside her, to blow away her doubts. But, as she paid for her coffee and went out again into the golden September sunshine, she knew that her delight in the morning had evaporated. And the scarlet rucksack and the new boots lying on the seat of the Mini seemed to have lost their magic.

Linzi was still in a thoughtful mood when she put on

her new boots and, carrying the light rucksack, set off up the valley after lunch. Perhaps up here, with the gorse and the heather clothing the mountains in their royal gold and purple, with ravens and buzzards circling high in the blue sky and larks and pipits singing their sweet songs, she would be able to sort out her tumultuous emotions and see a clear path ahead.

Her feelings about Richard were what worried her most. Until now, he had been the only man she had ever considered marrying. Surely that must mean *something*. He must have something to offer her that no other man had; something she both wanted and needed. And if it wasn't passion, was it to be so lightly thrown aside? Might it not be something more enduring, more valuable in the end?

Linzi reached the top of the track and paused to decide which way to go next. The track she was following led on across the hills, wide and clear—an old drovers' road, Jason had told her, which had once been a busy highway as the drovers brought their cattle across the mountains to the big markets. The journeys had been long and hard, and the cattle had been shod for the purpose; coming back, the drovers' dogs, often corgis bred for herding cattle, had been sent on ahead so that when they arrived home the women of the house would know that their menfolk would be back a few days later.

The romance of the old story appealed to Linzi and she decided to follow the track for another hour before turning back. There would be no danger of getting lost then, and she would note the appearance of the hills for further explorations.

She wondered who the man was who had spoken to Richard on the plane. Not one of Jason's friends, that was certain! But a man like Jason, with everything at his feet, was sure to have made a few enemies. And, particularly as he had remained unmarried, there were sure to be rumours about the women in his life. Linzi knew that there were bound to have been women—Jason was too masculine, too virile to have lived a celibate life. But was that any concern of hers? Or Richard's? And if it were true that Jason was a womaniser, wasn't it more important that Richard should trust her?

Linzi shied away from that question, which begged too many others. It was no use thinking about it anyway, she told herself fretfully. She could decide nothing until she had seen Jason again. And until then, why not enjoy this beautiful afternoon, the wild hills, the company of the big Alsatian who was bounding along like a puppy beside her. After all, there might not be that many more opportunities.

Putting her troubles aside for the moment, Linzi gazed around her. For the first time she really looked with attention at the mountains, noting their shapes, the power and strength of their outlines. Jason had told her that they were often his inspiration; many of the abstract forms he had carved had been suggested to him by the lines of the hills. He had shown her how they represented to him sculptures on the massive scale, the form delineated by the tracks that moved across them. The thrust of rock, the curves and hollows of the contours, the peaks and the valleys—all these could be seen in his studio, reproduced, with his own deep feelings for shape and form, his own affinity with the material, added to make something unique.

Only a man of deep sensitivity, Linzi realised, could express himself in this way. Could such a man be light and shallow in other ways? Could he be a mere womaniser, using the female body for his own instant physical satisfaction as well as for the translation of his ideas?

It was past teatime when she returned at last to Bron Melyn. Hugh was out and the house empty, but tea was laid on the terrace as usual. Linzi went through to the kitchen to put on the kettle and collect the plate of scones and bara brith left ready. The doorbell rang as she was making the tea, startling her, and she went through the hall to answer it.

The girl who stood there was a stranger to Linzi. Thin and pale, she had mousy hair and a face that was pretty without being outstanding. It was spoilt at the moment by a look of anxiety, a troubled shadow darkening the light blue eyes.

'Oh!' she said, looking startled. 'I'm sorry—I thought Mr Davies would answer.'

'Hugh's out. Can I do anything?' The girl was fidgeting with the handle of a small pram, Linzi noticed now. Surely she hadn't pushed it all the way up from Crickhowell? Perhaps she came from one of the isolated farms or cottages on the way.

'Well, it was Mr Carver I wanted to see really.' The girl's pale face flushed and she glanced involuntarily towards the pram. 'There was something—I need to talk to him.'

'I'm sorry, he's in Newport. He doesn't expect to be back until late, or possibly not even till tomorrow.' Linzi hesitated. 'Look, would you like a cup of tea? I'm just about to have one. You must have walked a long way, and it's such a hot afternoon. And then perhaps you could give me a message for Mr Carver.'

'Oh no, I couldn't—I mean, you must be busy, I——'

'No, I'm not, really.' Linzi smiled at her encouragingly. 'Do stay and have some tea with me. I've been on my own all day—I'd love to have someone to talk to.'

'Well—if you're sure.' The girl looked uncertainly at the pram. 'Can I put the baby in the shade somewhere?'

'Bring him through. Tea's out on the terrace—look, through here. It won't hurt to wheel the pram through. You settle yourself down and I'll be out straightaway.'

Still looking doubtful, the girl sat down on the edge of one of the chairs, while Linzi hurried back to the kitchen and set the teapot and cakes on a tray.

The girl puzzled her a little. She clearly felt herself to be out of her element at Bron Melyn, although equally clearly she was a local girl. Perhaps she had come about a job, Linzi thought, carrying the tray through to the terrace. In any case, she couldn't be sent back without some kind of refreshment; the poor kid—she didn't look much more than seventeen—looked just about ready to drop.

'Here we are,' Linzi announced, putting the tray down on the table. 'And I'm certainly ready for it! I've been miles this afternoon. Do you live near here—look, we don't even know each other's names! I'm Linzi Berwick.'

'My name's Sian,' the younger girl supplied. 'Sian Parry. You— you're not Linzi Berwick the model, are you?'

'Yes, I'm afraid so.' Linzi grinned ruefully. 'Sometimes I wish people wouldn't recognise me so instantly, then I wouldn't have to live up to what they expect of me. After all, I can't look much like your idea of a model just at the moment, in jeans and T-shirt!'

'I just wish I could look like that in jeans and T-shirt,' Sian said fervently. 'I never look anything but a mouse, whatever I wear.'

'But you could.' Linzi gazed critically at the fawn hair and large pale eyes, remembering how plain and gawky she had looked herself at this girl's age. 'You just need to learn how to make the best of yourself. I mean, you could do your hair differently, light up your eyes a bit—and a pink lipstick would work wonders. Tell you what, I'll give you a facial—some time when you're not busy, show you a few tricks of the trade.'

'*Would* you?' The girl was almost pathetically grateful. 'Not that anyone's going to notice round here. But still, you never know. . . .' Her voice and face were so wistful that Linzi felt a pang of sympathy. She'd been a rebel herself at this age—but she understood the longing to escape, to make a life of her own. Sian had probably never been away from the valley. Once she had, she would realise her good fortune in living here—but until then she would always yearn.

'Have you thought of getting a job away somewhere?'
she asked lightly, not wanting to interfere but unable to
resist showing some fellow-feeling. 'I went to London
when I was about your age. It's not a thing I'd advise
unless you already know people there—but I think it does
a girl good to leave home for a while.'

'Oh, I couldn't do that.' Sian shook her head decisively.
'There's David, you see.'

'David?' Linzi didn't understand. Then she saw the
faint flush on the girl's face and followed her glance to the
pram, where the baby was beginning to stir. 'You—you
mean that's *your* baby? I didn't realise—I thought you
must be just looking after him. I'm sorry—you don't look
old enough to be married!'

'I'm not married,' said Sian, her flush deepening.

'Oh lord,' Linzi said after a moment. 'I do put my
foot in it, don't I? I'm awfully sorry, Sian. I just didn't
think——'

'It's all right,' Sian said quietly. 'I'm pretty well used
to it now. Oh, it wouldn't seem anything to you, coming
from London—but round here people are still a bit—well,
old-fashioned, I suppose you'd say.'

'I see.' Linzi gazed at her. She must have had a pretty rot-
ten time; no wonder she looked as pale and scared as a little
mouse. 'And there's no chance of the—the father——'

'Oh, he won't marry me,' Sian said, bitterness showing
itself in her voice for the first time. 'I'm not his type. Not
for marriage anyway. All right for——' She left the words
unsaid, but Linzi felt another quick stab of sympathy.
Poor kid, she'd been too young to know what it was all
about. The baby looked about three months old. Who
had been selfish enough to take advantage of this child a
year ago? One of the local lads, presumably. Well, she
hoped Sian was making sure he was helping to support
his child, at least. Though whatever he was giving her, it
couldn't be enough or she wouldn't be looking for work
now.

'Look,' she said, 'I'm sure Mr Carver will help you. And I'll put in a word for you. I'm sure Megan could do with some help in the house. I expect you could even bring the baby with you. Why don't you come back the day after tomorrow? I'll have had time to tell him about you by then.'

Sian stared at her, a strange expression on her face. For a few moments Linzi wondered if the girl was, after all, backward in some way. She just didn't seem to understand what had been said. Then the pale face cleared and a second deep flush stained the cheeks. The girl looked wildly at Linzi, then at the pram and back again.

'Oh no!' she exclaimed. 'You've got it all wrong! I didn't come for a *job*! I wanted to see—I have to talk to Mr Carver about——' Her eyes went back to the pram; but before she could say any more there was a sound from inside the house, and the next moment they both looked round as Ceri Penrhys came through the patio doors, dressed in a swirling cotton skirt of brilliant emerald green and a white peasant blouse that showed her curving figure off to its full advantage.

'I just thought I'd call in to ask you——' she began gaily, as Linzi felt herself turn cold. And then she stopped. Her dark eyes fell on Sian, looked past her to the pram, and narrowed angrily.

'And just what are *you* doing here?' she asked, her tone low and vicious. 'Currying favour? I suppose you thought you'd find Jason at home, try to get around him? Well, *Miss* Parry, you thought wrong, didn't you? So you'd better be going—back where you came from. And don't let me see you round here again!' Her glance swept over the pram and there was a look of contempt in her eyes. 'You got everything you deserve, my girl, and you're not getting an ounce more—from anyone.'

The flush had ebbed away from Sian's cheeks, leaving

her white and ghostly. Linzi saw the tears in the girl's eyes as she rose hastily and took hold of the pram handle, and she leapt up to restrain her, furious at Ceri's interference.

'No, Sian, you don't have to go! You haven't finished your tea—sit down again.' She whipped round to face Ceri. 'I don't know who you think you are, coming here and giving the orders——'

'And *I* don't know who you think *you* are!' Ceri cut in. 'You're just an employee here, right? A model. *I'm* a close friend of the owner of this house and I know who he wants here and who he doesn't. And this—this *trash*—' her lip curled disdainfully '—isn't one of the people he wants. So get going,' she added, addressing Sian again, 'and don't come back until you're invited!'

Her face burning, Sian turned away. She wheeled the pram along the terrace and disappeared round the corner, while Linzi watched helplessly. She had no way of knowing whether Ceri's words were true—but she made up her mind she'd find out as soon as Jason came home.

But it seemed that Ceri had thought of that too, and had no intention of letting it happen. She watched Sian's exit with a malevolent expression, then turned to Linzi with an entirely different look on her face—a complacent, conspiratorial look, as if to suggest that she and Linzi were on one side, and Sian and her like firmly on the other.

'I'm sorry you had to be pestered with her,' she said warmly. 'I suppose you thought I was a bit harsh—but you have to be with a girl of that type, or there's no knowing where it will end. Anyway, I don't think she'll be coming back here. Just as well Jason wasn't here, though!' she laughed.

'But I don't understand,' Linzi said in bewilderment. 'Why did she come? What did she want? I thought she wanted work—but she said not. She said she wanted to see Jason, to talk to him.' She stopped suddenly, an unpleasant suspicion entering her mind.

'I bet she did,' Ceri agreed. 'And can't you guess why? She wants to pin that baby on him! Well, she could be right at that—though I've never known Jason slip up before—but I'd be very surprised if there weren't quite a few other candidates as well. Little Sian's just starting at the top—but she's not going to get anywhere, not if I have anything to do with it!'

'The *baby*? *Jason*? But surely——'

'Why not?' Ceri's eyes were bright with malice. 'I've never supposed Jason lived like a monk, have you? And I was away all last summer, doing some TV. I hope I'm realistic enough not to expect a man to live an unnatural life—though of course, as soon as we're properly engaged things will be rather different.'

Linzi shook her head in bewilderment. Ceri's reasoning was beyond her. She seemed to accept quite naturally that Jason *could* be the father of Sian's baby—yet had denied categorically to the girl that he would raise a finger to help her. Her attitude seemed to be quite ambivalent, and totally callous as far as Sian and her child were concerned. As for herself, Linzi didn't know what to think. It was yet another puzzle to add to the turmoil in her mind.

'Anyway, don't let's talk about Sian,' Ceri went on. 'Look, I really came over to— well, to apologise for last night. I know I wasn't really fair to you. But just imagine how *you'd* feel if your fiancé was having a beautiful model living in the house with him!' She laughed gaily. 'I'm afraid the little green-eyed monster took over for a while! But you won't hold it against me, will you? I'd really like to be friends.'

Linzi looked at her. The pretty face was open and confiding, warmth and friendliness shone from the dark eyes. Was the older girl to be trusted or not? Linzi sighed and gave up. It could hardly matter, anyway. She was so confused that she could hardly trust herself, let alone anyone else.

'And I came over to invite you and Jason to dinner on Friday,' Ceri went on. 'You'll never guess what's happening—Selwyn's going to be home. Well, we knew he was coming, but we didn't expect it to be so quick. He'll be here tomorrow, isn't it marvellous? It's months since we've had him home, so naturally we want to celebrate. And I do want you to meet him before you go back to London.'

So that was it, Linzi thought. Selwyn was to be the distraction, removing temptation from Jason. Well, it could make no difference, and there was nothing she could do about it anyway. She smiled back at Ceri and said she couldn't speak for Jason, but if it was all right with him she'd love to come.

'That's fine, then.' Ceri stood up gracefully. 'Perhaps you'll get Jason to ring me to fix a time. And I'll have to be getting back now—there's a heap to do before Selwyn comes!' She smiled up at Linzi as the taller girl stood up too. 'I'm glad we're friends. I really don't know what got into me last night! But everything's all right now, isn't it?'

'Oh yes,' said Linzi, walking round to the front of the house with her, 'everything's all right now.'

And that's the biggest lie you ever told, Linzi Berwick, she thought, walking slowly back to the terrace. Because when she sorted it all out, it seemed that there was very little that was all right. The confusing events of the day chased disturbingly through her mind. Richard's call—Sian—Ceri—what was the truth of anything?

Her mind came back to Sian and the baby, a new and disturbing element in the puzzle. *Was* it—could it be—Jason's? She hadn't seen the child clearly, he had been asleep. But her memory brought a fresh jolt as she pictured again the tiny head emerging from the blankets. The crinkled face. The mop of hair.

The mop of thick, black hair.

CHAPTER SIX

Jason returned late that night. Linzi was in bed, but still awake, and she heard the grey Lancia sweep into the yard, its lights bringing a momentary glow to her curtains. Restlessly she turned over, unable to decide whether she was glad or sorry that he had come back. Tomorrow she would have to meet him, with all her new-found knowledge, and she just didn't have any idea how to handle the situation.

However, she thought as she dressed for breakfast, there was no way to avoid it, so she might as well use all the morale-boosters she had. And, tired of leotard and jeans, she dressed in a full white skirt patterned with swirling black, and a close-fitting black T shirt. Her tawny hair she left loose, swinging in a curving bell around her cheeks, and she applied only a dusting of make-up and just enough pink lipstick to emphasise the full curves of her mouth.

Jason was already on the terrace when she arrived. Once again, the September morning was perfect; just a hint of coolness in the air that came with the pearly mist, enough for Linzi to shrug her shoulders into a vivid green shawl, but with the same golden promise of a warm day that had been Bron Melyn's welcome to her ever since she had arrived. The weather must break soon, she mused, taking her seat and looking warily across the table at Jason, but so far there were no signs of it.

She had decided to leave all the running to Jason. Whatever he had meant by his words two nights ago, it was up to him to take the matter further if he wanted to. It was quite possible that he'd thought things over in the cold light of day and regretted his actions. In any case, she reflected ruefully, she was like a lamb with a lion as far as Jason was concerned; whatever their encounter, he was likely to emerge the winner.

'Hi,' said Jason, looking up with a smile that turned her heart over. 'You look very nice this morning.' His eyes lingered on the curves so flatteringly revealed by the snug T-shirt. 'Aren't we doing any work, then?'

'I can change after breakfast,' Linzi said shortly. She tried not to notice his own dark good looks and the muscular power of his body in the tan slacks and shirt. 'You don't look exactly dressed in your old clothes yourself,' she added.

'Like you, I thought I'd be civilised for once,' he agreed smoothly. 'Did you have a good day yesterday?'

Oh yes, Linzi wanted to answer bitterly. Just a phone call all the way from Vienna to tell me of your reputation, and confirmation in the afternoon in the shape of a baby and a distraught young mother. . . . She wondered what Jason's reaction would be to that, and decided not to risk it.

'I took Bracken up on the hill for a walk in the afternoon,' she said noncommittally. 'Wearing proper boots this time—I went into Crickhowell in the morning to buy them.'

'Did you indeed?' His eyes widened. 'Well, so my words do have some effect on you after all. You must have changed in the past five years!'

'I should hope I had,' she retorted. 'I shouldn't like to think I was still as gullible as I was then.'

'Meaning?' The warmth had gone from his eyes, leaving them chilled and wary.

'Meaning you took me in once, and you aren't likely to do it again,' Linzi said levelly. 'I'm only thankful that I saw the light in time five years ago. Marriage between us would never have worked, Jason—I knew it then and it's even more clear to me now.'

She poured herself a cup of coffee, wishing that her hand wouldn't shake as she did so. Jason's eyes were on her trembling fingers, she knew; looking up, she saw his glance travel insolently over her body, and her face flamed as she remembered the last time he had seen her.

'I don't remember mentioning marriage to you just lately,' he murmured at last, and she flinched at the implication. 'But I certainly got the impression that you were more than willing for—shall we say a somewhat closer relationship than we've enjoyed until now? Or was I wrong?'

'Maybe we were both wrong,' Linzi replied crisply, though inside she was shaking. 'All right, Jason, you're an attractive man. But you don't need me to tell you that, do you? You can get confirmation of that whenever you like. From Ceri, certainly—and from others, when Ceri's not around.'

'And just what do you mean by that, exactly?' he snapped.

'I think you know quite well what I mean.' Bravely, Linzi met his eyes, though the ice in them stabbed her to the heart. 'I realise it's too much to expect a man like you to manage without women entirely, Jason. But I do think you could confine your pleasures to those who are experienced enough to share them with you, and I think you could be a little more responsible too. Leaving an innocent teenager in the lurch just isn't funny. At least, I don't think so.'

The sapphire eyes widened and turned a slate-blue as Jason stared at her. Then the black brows came down over them in a scowl that had Linzi cringing in her seat. The lines deepened and brought a cruel harshness to the craggy face as Jason said in a low, dangerous tone:

'Just what are you talking about, Linzi? Would you mind coming out into the open and explaining some of these accusations you seem set on making? And telling me just what went on yesterday to cause all this? I thought when I went away that we'd begun to come to some sort of understanding. Now it seems I was wrong.'

'Yes, you were, weren't you?' Linzi was quaking now, wishing she'd never started the argument, wondering how she could get away without having to say any more. She'd seen Jason angry before, plenty of times; but never seen quite that look in his eyes, that hardness to his mouth.

'So? I'm waiting for your explanation, Linzi.'

Desperate, Linzi took refuge in the age-old cry of women everywhere. 'If you don't know, I'm certainly not telling you!' Half rising from her chair, she backed away, not knowing what Jason would do next. 'And I can't believe that you don't know—or maybe you just don't know which particular girl I'm referring to—maybe there are so many of them that——'

There was a sudden harsh squeal as Jason scraped his chair back on the stone flags of the terrace and came towards her. Terrified now, Linzi turned to run, but he had her before she had gone a yard, and wrenched her round to face him. His eyes were like stones as they glared down at her, and as she turned her head to escape their fury he brought one hand up to her chin, twisting her head brutally so that she was forced to look at him.

'Now,' he grated, 'maybe you'll tell me just where you picked up all this juicy gossip!'

Linzi closed her eyes and shook her head weakly. She couldn't say any more, she couldn't. She wanted only that he should let her go, let her escape the terrifying, disturbing nearness of his body, from the virile masculinity that assaulted her senses and weakened her knees. She wished desperately that she'd taken Richard's advice and never come here; or at least left yesterday, before all this torment began.

'I—I can't,' she whispered brokenly. 'I'm sorry—I should never have said anything.'

'You're darned right you shouldn't,' he said grimly. 'And one of these fine days I'll get the whole truth out of you, my girl.' His fingers tightened on her arms. 'I must say, it's nice to know you trust me so implicitly. At least I know enough now not to make any mistakes of my own! I just could have done that.' He let her go abruptly, and Linzi staggered. 'All right. We'll call it a day, shall we? And maybe we'd better both go and change for work. I'd like to get ahead as fast as possible now.'

And it was quite obvious why, Linzi thought as she went up the stairs to her bedroom. Whatever there might have been between her and Jason had been destroyed by this morning's scene. She admitted to herself that she could, if Jason had shown any signs of loving her, have accepted the fact of Sian and her baby—provided that Jason had looked after them properly. But the indications were that he had no such intention. That he was denying responsibility and had enlisted Ceri's help in sending the girl packing. And that was something Linzi couldn't stomach.

Jason must have realised this, and seen too that any chance of an affair with her was now over. From now on, their relationship would be strictly professional—and terminated as soon as possible.

The next few days passed slowly, Linzi realised for the first time that ever since she had arrived she and Jason had been building up a companionable relationship; a 'togetherness' that allowed them to share a comfortable silence, a mental communication that enabled them to understand the other's thoughts without a lot of explanation. Jason's work had helped with this growing understanding, for in the studio they were both professional, with no strains or embarrassment, and this ease had carried over into their everyday life. It had, Linzi thought, paved the way for the acknowledgement of her love.

Now, that companionship and understanding seemed to have vanished. They still worked together, but without the sense of sharing that there had been before. Linzi felt shut out, a mere dummy, as Jason examined and measured her with the indifferent air of a bricklayer rather than a sculptor. Remembering how emotionally involved he usually was in his work, she wondered if it would make any difference to the final figure, but dared not ask him. This new, remote Jason would be more likely to pretend that he didn't know what she was talking about than to answer her truthfully.

On the Friday evening they both went to dinner at Penrhys Court. Linzi would infinitely have preferred not to go—she wasn't staying long, she pointed out when Jason received the invitation, she hardly knew the family (and didn't much like Ceri anyway, she added silently) and could only be an intruder on a family celebration. But Jason had ignored her reluctance, telling her curtly that she had been invited, and that was that. Besides, it wasn't often that someone new came to the valley and old Mr Penrhys had seemed to take to her. 'Though I can't say I'm sorry you won't be here long enough for him to find out what you're really like, he had added caustically, and Linzi had been too depressed even to defend herself.

She still had enough pride, however, to take pains with her appearance when Friday came. She looked into her wardrobe, thankful that she had brought two evening dresses with her; the sea-green Grecian style she had worn before, when Ceri came, so it had to be the other and she took it out and looked it over critically. In a deep golden-brown velvet, with shawl collar and nipped-in waist above the billowing skirt, it was ideal for the cooler evenings and brought out the auburn lights in her smooth hair. A heavy gold neck-chain and matching bracelet glowed against her tanned skin, and she decided that plain gold ear-rings would look better than more elaborate ones. Gold sandals completed her outfit and she stood back from the mirror feeling that at least she was doing herself justice. She pushed away the rueful wish that it would have been nice to be doing Jason justice too. . . .

Not that he needed anyone to do him justice. He was dressed as immaculately as on the previous occasion, and once more his appearance made her heart miss a beat. No wonder Ceri had set her mind on capturing him, she thought dully as he led her out to the car; no wonder poor little Sian had been overwhelmed! And her own treacherous senses were saved by a sharp jolt of anger. He *shouldn't* have deserted that poor child, and she only wished she had the courage to tell him so!

She settled herself in the car and Jason slid into the driver's seat. His nearness sent a tingle through her limbs and she glanced sideways at him in an effort to gauge his reaction. But he seemed totally unmoved, his profile harsh and stern as he looked straight ahead. And when he spoke it was to utter only stilted small-talk, evidently in an attempt to bring about a more normal atmosphere between them before they arrived at the Court.

He doesn't want me here any more than I want to be here, Linzi thought miserably, and wondered just how long it would be before she was able to return to London.

The journey to Penrhys Court was short, although it involved winding through a maze of tiny lanes. Linzi had realised soon after arriving at Bron Melyn that there were several such ways branching from the lane leading to the studio. She had wandered along some of them on free afternoons, but felt that it would be easier to get lost among them than on the hills themselves. She watched idly as the headlights lit up banks and hedgerows. The evenings were drawing in now; it was dark by seven-thirty and the drop in temperature then signified that the Indian summer was almost at an end and that autumn would soon give way to winter.

Penrhys Court was ablaze with lights as they turned up the gravel drive. Linzi looked at it with interest. It had obviously been a grand house once, fitted to belong to the local landowner—did they have squires in Wales? Now, as Mr Penrhys had admitted to her the other day, lack of money meant that it wasn't maintained to its previous standards. But at night it still looked beautiful, and Linzi's imagination supplied a row of carriages standing outside the door, with grandly dressed ladies and gentlemen making their way to the festivities within.

Tonight, however, it was just she and Jason getting out of the car. She was glad of her long dress, which gave a semblance of romance to the scene, and glanced with new appreciation at Jason's dinner-jacket. The old house needn't be too insulted after all, she thought, and smiled.

'Something amusing you?' Jason's voice was clipped and Linzi felt sad that they couldn't share even this simple joke. A few days ago, they would have done, and she realised again just how far apart they had drifted.

She was saved from replying by the front door swinging open and Ceri's high voice calling down to them. She sounded excited, Linzi thought, but of course she would be, with her twin brother home for the first time in a year. For a moment she closed her eyes; she had almost forgotten Selwyn, so recently returned from New York. But New York was a big place, it was hardly likely he'd have heard of her there. And he would be too happy to be at home to take much notice of a girl who was only here for a few weeks anyway.

'So lovely to see you!' Ceri gushed as they went into the brightness of the panelled hall. 'Let me take your cloak, Linzi. . . . Well, anyone could see that *you* know about clothes, you look ravishing. Doesn't she, Jason? I'm afraid you put me absolutely in the shade—good thing I haven't got a jealous nature!'

Linzi glanced at her and felt her lips twitch. Evidently Ceri was to be the sweet, simple girl-next-door tonight— in manner, anyway. Her clothes certainly didn't give that impression, and Linzi doubted very much whether Jason thought that Ceri was overshadowed by her own appearance. Indeed, as she looked at him she could see by his appreciative expression that he didn't.

Ceri was wearing a dress of brilliant turquoise in a clinging jersey that left little to the imagination. The neckline plunged to show the deep valley between her soft, full breasts, and her eyes sparkled with mischief as she glanced knowingly from Linzi to Jason.

'You must come in and meet Selwyn,' she went on, taking them each by one hand and guiding them into a long, elegant drawing-room. There was no sign of lack of money here, Linzi thought, but perhaps the Penrhys family had decided that whatever the rest of the house was like, the public rooms were to remain as they should be, as they had always been—an epitome of luxury and good taste. And they were certainly that; she couldn't help admiring the furniture, the carpets and pictures. Firelight glowed on the dark old panelling; once again she had a vision of those elegant people from long ago, grouped about the room like characters from a Jane Austen novel.

Mr Penrhys was sitting at one end of a comfortably overstuffed chesterfield. He got up as Linzi and Jason entered, and she took his hand, smiling at him and murmuring a few complimentary comments about the house. Then she turned to meet the other occupant of the room, and was conscious that her heart was already beating fast.

'So you're Linzi Berwick,' Selwyn Penrhys remarked lazily. He was very much like his twin sister, his dark hair curling over his forehead. Brown eyes looked quizzically into hers, his mouth smiled with practised charm. 'Well, I sure didn't expect to find a top international model living next door when I came home. What's Jason's secret?'

'No secret,' Linzi answered lightly, aware of Jason's sombre eyes on her. 'He just needed a model and I happened to fill the bill.'

'And a very nice filling too,' Selwyn drawled. He was much taller than Ceri, only inches shorter than Jason. He had picked up a twang of American in his travels and his voice was attractively deep. 'Ceri tells me you knew each other as kids too.'

'That's right. My parents took Jason in when he was just a toddler. I didn't come along for quite a few years after that, of course—Jason was almost grown-up before I arrived on the scene.'

'Kinda big brother, hey?' The American seemed a little overstressed then, but Selwyn's smile took away any slight irritation there might have been. 'Well, I envy him his choice in kid sisters!' He glanced at Ceri and grinned. 'Not that I've got anything to complain about in that department!'

Ceri came over and hugged his arm. 'You're not so bad as brothers go, either,' she offered. 'Except that you're not here often enough.'

'Well, someone has to make the money,' he answered mildly. 'Look, what'll you have to drink, Linzi? Martini? It's still Scotch for Jason, I guess?'

'Please. With lemonade,' she added, watching him go over to a drinks trolley that seemed to be supplied with almost every drink under the sun. Once again she became aware of Jason watching her and looked up to find his eyes fixed on her with a sardonic light in their depths. Flushing a little, she turned away and smiled deliberately at Selwyn as he handed her her drink.

'You've been in New York until recently, haven't you?' he enquired, his dark eyes already beginning their flirtation. 'I daresay Ceri's told you I've just come over from there. We must have a talk some time—may find we've got some mutual friends.'

'Yes, we must.' Linzi's heart had bumped uncomfortably at his first words, but there seemed to be nothing sinister behind them and she gave herself a stern little talking-to. New York was a *big* place. Millions of people lived and worked there. She must stop this silly panic whenever the place was mentioned. . . .

'. . . . getting on with the figure?' she heard, and blinked at Selwyn.

'I'm sorry—I didn't catch what you said.'

He laughed. 'I was just asking how Jason was getting on with the figure. It's to be quite a masterpiece, apparently. Have people flocking to see it once it's in position.'

'I don't know if sculpture ever gets quite that mass reaction,' Linzi said slowly. 'People don't seem to realise just what goes into it, on the whole. They look at a piece of marble or a bronze, and they either appreciate only its photographic qualities, if it's a straight representation, or they wrinkle their noses and just pass it by if it's abstract. They don't see the form, the line, the shape it makes of the air around it. They don't understand the magic of it; what you can *do* with its curves and hollows and its mass. It doesn't say anything to their imaginations.' She sipped her drink. 'Since I've been here I've been looking at the hills and the valleys—all massive sculptures in themselves. But translate that into something in a studio, something you can pick up and handle, and it seems to leave a lot of people cold.'

'I don't understand it, but I know what I like,' Selwyn suggested, and Linzi laughed and nodded.

Feeling at ease for the first time for several days, she turned to smile at Mr Penrhys—and caught Jason's glance. He was sitting beside the old man, deep in talk, but they were both looking in her direction. She didn't know if Jason had heard her words or not. But for a moment his eyes were unguarded, and their expression was one she'd never seen in them before. Inexplicably embarrassed, she turned away, and caught an odd look passing between Ceri and her brother, a look of understanding and mutual compliance.

Linzi shook herself. She finished her drink and turned back to Selwyn. He was looking pensive—perhaps he hadn't expected a model to have thoughts of her own. But he said nothing more on the subject of sculpture, and their talk drifted into other channels. Linzi found him a pleasant, easy man to talk to. But her feeling of disquiet persisted and she was relieved when Ceri at last announced that dinner was ready and they all moved slowly out of the room.

Ceri had done most of the cooking herself, Linzi discovered, helped by the young girl who served the food. It was surprisingly good—though why she should be surprised that Ceri could cook, Linzi wasn't really sure. Not many people could afford to employ full-time cooks these days, and the Penrhys family almost certainly couldn't. She could see why Ceri was so keen to marry Jason; his work was now bringing in a very handsome income, and no doubt he could work as well at Penrhys Court as at Bron Melyn. She could see the sense of such an arrangement. Penrhys was certainly worth putting money into and would make a fitting home for a famous sculptor. But she felt sad at the idea of Bron Melyn being let or sold.

After dinner, they went back to the drawing-room. Old Mr Penrhys, who had eaten little, declared his intention of going to bed early. Ceri seized the opportunity to invite Jason to see some old prints that had been unearthed in one of the attics. And Linzi found herself alone with Selwyn.

'Well, we'll just have to try to amuse ourselves, won't we,' he drawled, looking as if he could think of several ways to accomplish this. 'Anyone ever tell you you're a beautiful girl, Linzi?'

'I *am* a model,' she answered drily. 'It's all very subjective, of course—depends entirely on one's own idea of beauty.'

'Well, I should say you were most men's.' He brought her a liqueur and sat down close to her on the chesterfield. 'Certainly mine, anyway, and that's the only opinion I care about. How do you get on with the famous stonemason, then? Must be strange, getting together after all these years.'

Linzi slanted a glance up at him. She wasn't sure just how much he knew. 'Jason and I work very well together,' she rejoined primly. 'And I'm not sure how he'd react to hearing you call him a stonemason.'

Selwyn laughed easily. 'Oh, that's just my joke. Jay and I understand one another.... I suppose, you being more of a kid sister to him, your relationship'd be a bit different from most.'

Linzi hesitated. 'I don't know quite what you mean.' ·

'Oh, don't act the innocent, it doesn't suit you.' The dark eyes were roving over her. 'Most girls who looked like you wouldn't stand a chance with Jay Carver living in the same house. I mean, you're practically alone there with him, aren't you, and Hugh wouldn't see anything Jason didn't want him to see.' He moved a little nearer. 'Well? *Are* you still his kid sister? Or has time made a few changes here and there?'

'Jason and I have a working relationship,' Linzi retorted. 'I don't know what you're trying to tell me, Mr——'

'Selwyn—you called me that all through dinner, why stop now?'

'All right, *Selwyn*—or what you're trying to imply, but I can assure you that it's nothing more than that, nothing at all!'

'Well, okay, that's fine.' The eyes were almost undressing her now and she shifted abruptly away along the chesterfield. 'You're engaged anyway, so Ceri tells me, so I'm sure you wouldn't want it any other way. But we all need a bit of comfort now and then, and I should think it's pretty lonely for you, with your boy-friend away, isn't it?' He let his hand move gently over her shoulder, the fingertips reaching over the collar to caress her bare skin. Linzi got quickly to her feet.

'I can stand being lonely, thank you.' She wished Jason would come back. She ought to be able to handle this importunate Welshman, but for some reason he frightened her.

'Well, I'm sure you can.' Selwyn was on his feet too,

moving close against her. 'And I wouldn't ask you to do anything you didn't want to do. But there's no harm in a little fun, is there? Between friends, and no strings or hard feelings when it's over?' He slid his hands up her arms and before she could stop him his mouth was on hers, forceful and demanding. A tide of fury and repugnance rose in Linzi, flooding body and limbs as she struggled, but Selwyn merely laughed softly in his throat and held her closer, his arms hard around her shoulders, his finger-tips probing under her arms to find her breasts. She felt his teeth against her lips and jerked her head back, and felt rather than heard his stifled curse as one hand came up behind her head to hold it while he bent her body back over his arm. Her own hands flailed uselessly behind him, trapped almost to the wrist, unable to do more than claw at the back of his jacket. With a swift movement he twisted her round to the chesterfield and bore her down upon it, his weight forcing her back against the cushions. Linzi gave a cry of fear as she felt his hand fumbling with her dress, then sagged with relief as she heard someone at the door.

Selwyn jerked himself off her as the door opened, but there wasn't time for Linzi to do more than struggle into a sitting position and raise her hands to her disordered hair. It must have been quite obvious to the two who came in that something had been going on; and it was inevitable that they should misunderstand.

'Well, you and Selwyn do seem to be hitting it off!' Ceri exclaimed with a gurgle. 'Sorry if we came back too soon—Jason did say he was sure you'd be all right, but I didn't like to leave you on your own too long.' She sent a sideways look at Jason. 'And you see, you were right, weren't you? We could have stayed a lot longer. But still, it's not really polite, is it?' Her eyes came back to Linzi, noting the crumpled dress and disarranged hair. 'I hope Selwyn hasn't been too naughty—you have to be stern with him, his girl-friends all tell me!'

Colour flamed in Linzi's cheeks. She looked away from Ceri's suggestive glance and found Jason's eyes on her, dark with some unfathomable emotion, the lines of his face etched deeply with anger and something else—it could have been disgust, but she didn't want to believe that. Surely *he* must realise that whatever Selwyn had been doing, she wouldn't have been encouraging him. But as she gazed at him, mutely begging him to understand, he turned away. As if dismissing her, she thought, stung; as if considering her beneath contempt.

'Now, what shall we do?' Ceri cried gaily. 'Do you play cards, Linzi? Oh, not bridge or anything madly intelligent like that—but whist? Solo? Would you like a game?'

Well, it was a way of passing the evening, Linzi thought as they gathered round a table. At least it would keep conversation to a minimum and she wouldn't be exposed to any more embarrassment from Selwyn. But as her eyes met Jason's when she raised them from the cards, or their fingers touched accidentally as he passed her a drink, she knew that her discomfort wasn't by any means over. If Jason's thunderous expression was anything to go by, it had only just begun. And she dreaded the drive back to Bron Melyn.

A dread that proved to have good reason behind it. Almost as soon as Jason had started the car and they were moving down the drive, with Ceri and Selwyn still waving in the doorway, he began.

'Just what was going on in the drawing-room while Ceri and I were upstairs?'

Linzi was too tired and unhappy to choose her words. 'What do you mean, going on? I could just as well ask what was going on upstairs!'

He brushed that aside. 'When we came in, Selwyn was by the fire looking as if he'd just run a mile and you were on the chesterfield, and you didn't look as if you'd been sitting quietly discussing the weather. Your hair was all over the place, your skirt up to your knees— '

'So what?' she flashed, knowing that he'd never believe the truth. 'Just what business is it of yours anyway? I don't have to answer to you for what I do!'

'You're living in my house, under my care——' Jason began, but Linzi, her temper really roused now, interrupted him again.

'I'm *not* under your care! I haven't been for the past five years. That's all over, remember, finished. My God, I was right to run out when I did—I dread to think what life would have been like with you. Why, you'd probably have chained me up during the day so that I couldn't get into any mischief. And as for leading my own life in any way at all——'

'You're dead right there' he gritted. 'I'd probably have *had* to chain you up! The way you've been behaving since you came to Bron Melyn, I'd never have had a minute's peace any other way. I wonder just how many times you'd have betrayed me by now——'

Infuriated, Linzi turned and slashed her hand across his face, regardless of the fact that he was still driving, even though slowly. At once he slammed on the brakes and the car jerked to a halt. In the dim light she could see that his face was twisted with rage, and she instinctively cringed away in her seat.

'Why, you stupid little fool!' There was a note of contempt in his voice that stabbed at her heart. 'What in God's name do you think you're doing?' His hand shot out and grasped her wrist, wrenching painfully at the fine skin. 'You deserve a thorough good hiding for that, and I'm darned if one of these fine days I won't give it to you. I've been itching to teach you a lesson for years.' The threat tore at her nerves. 'You think you can do just what you like, don't you, and just because you've got the kind of looks most men go mad for you've got away with it up till now. But not any longer, sweet Linzi. What is it they call you? The Swan?' His fingers came up to encircle her slender neck and she could feel the tactile strength in them, the tension of fury that quivered against her skin. 'You really do play with fire, don't you,' he murmured, his voice dangerously silky now. 'You really do. . . . But it's not for much longer, little girl. Not for much longer.' The fingertips stroked gently at her neck, the thumbs meeting in the hollow of her throat, and Linzi closed her eyes in fear. There had always been this hidden streak of violence in Jason, but surely . . .? She made a tremendous effort and opened her eyes again, meeting his though she quailed before the open anger in them.

'Look, I don't know what brought all this on,' she managed to whisper. 'A kiss—is that what you're objecting to? Selwyn's an attractive man—Ceri's an attractive girl. You have your fun, why shouldn't I have mine?' Her courage ebbed back as Jason let his hands drop from her neck and sat there staring at her. 'And you're no one to talk anyway, Jason Carver. What about Sian? What about that poor child and the baby you've landed her with? Or did you think that had been sufficiently hushed up?' Cautiously, she shifted away from him, almost petrifyingly afraid of his reaction yet unable to stem the flow of words. 'You think I'm contemptible, don't you,' she threw at him, her voice cutting. 'Just because you found me and Selwyn looking as if we'd been—been kissing, you think I'm beyond the pale. Well, whatever you think of me, it's just *nothing* to what *I* think of *you*! Anyone who could do what you did—seduce an innocent child, who couldn't have been much over sixteen at the time—land her with a baby you refused to acknowledge—and then try to make out she was promiscuous anyway and the baby could belong to half a dozen different men—well, if what I've done is contemptible, there just isn't any word for *that*! It's a pity the days of horsewhips and shotguns seem to have gone, Jason, because if anyone deserved them, you do!'

The silence in the car after she had finished was almost tangible. Linzi kept her eyes on Jason's for as long as she could, trembling uncontrollably at the darkening expres-

sion, the seething anger that she saw there. Obviously
he'd thought she didn't know about that, thought her
accusations the other day were wild and empty. Now he
knew—and she was aware that his fury transcended anything she'd yet seen.

'So that's it,' Jason growled at last. 'That's what's been
festering in your mind these past few days. And I suppose
you concocted this pretty little tale while I was in Newport
the other day. Just why, I wonder? Because you were
afraid of what you were getting yourself into? Because
you were afraid of your own response to me? Don't trouble
to deny it—you know very well you were ready to melt
into my arms that night, you'd have been mine without a
second thought for your precious Richard if I'd persisted.
Even now—' his fingers reached out to touch her neck
and slid down inside the collar of her dress to stroke the
rounded breasts beneath '—even now, if I wanted to make
love to you, you'd let me. Oh, you might struggle at first—'
his hand tightened as she pulled ineffectually at his arm
'—but you'd come in the end. Wouldn't you, my darling?'
The word was invested with contempt as he moved closer
and his lips met hers in a hard, brief kiss. 'Don't worry,
Linzi. I'm not going to have my wicked way with you—
not tonight, anyway. And you needn't make up any more
fairy-tales to keep your precious virginity inviolate. I
imagine the one you've just recounted will be more than
enough to keep you safe until I've finished my work.'

'Fairy-tale?' Linzi held desperately to the shreds of dignity that were all she had left. 'That's no fairy-tale,
Jason—and you needn't try to convince me it is. I've *seen*
that baby—and nothing will persuade me that it isn't
yours, nothing!'

His eyes raked her body, leaving her feeling that she'd
been stripped naked. For a moment his barely-suppressed
anger seemed to fill the car almost to exploding point.
Then he turned away, and started the engine again.

'There's no more to be said then, is there?' he snarled;

and Linzi felt herself grow cold. She hadn't meant to say that — it wasn't even true, not entirely. She'd just wanted to lash out—to hurt him as deeply as she herself had been hurt. For a moment she longed to call the words back, to have them unsaid; but a glance at Jason's white, furious face told her that no apology could take back what she had just done to him.

Jason didn't speak again all the way home. Nor when he let Linzi out of the car and saw her into the house. Nor when he turned abruptly away and went out again, slamming the door behind him and making his way with heavy tread across the yard to the studio.

CHAPTER SEVEN

Jason did not appear at breakfast the next morning. As if in accordance with their stormy relationship, the weather had broken, and Hugh brought Linzi's coffee and grapefruit into the little breakfast-room just off the kitchen. It faced east to catch the morning sun, but there wasn't any sun to catch this morning. The sky had darkened and brooding clouds hung low over the hilltops. Linzi looked out of the window and shivered.

'Isn't Jason eating breakfast?' she enquired with an attempt at nonchalance, but Hugh was impassive as he poured coffee.

'He's already had his—said he wanted to get to work early. He's very much absorbed when he's working.'

'Yes, I know.'

'Did you enjoy the dinner-party last night? Selwyn Penrhys is back, I believe.'

'Yes, that's right. Do you know him, Hugh?'

'Not well.' Hugh's face was guarded. 'He's been here, of course. Jason's more—friendly—with his sister, and of course Selwyn has been away a lot.'

'Yes, so I understand.' So Hugh didn't like Selwyn either, Linzi thought, and wondered why. She'd told herself it was just her own unhappy association with New York, plus Selwyn's pass at her which he might very well regret now. But there was something else. . . .

Jason didn't want her in the studio this morning, Hugh had told her, and she was at something of a loose end when, shortly before eleven, Megan came out to where she was helping Alun with some gardening to tell her she had a visitor. Puzzled, Linzi followed her indoors, wiping her hands on her handkerchief as she did so, and found Selwyn lounging near the patio door.

'Oh,' Linzi said blankly. 'Megan told me it was someone for me, shall I fetch Jason?'

Selwyn smiled. 'But I *am* for you, Linzi—how could you doubt it? No, it wasn't Jason I wanted to see.' He studied her. 'I wanted to ask you to have dinner with me. Tonight. I want to get to know you, Linzi.'

'You do?' Linzi remembered the previous night. 'I thought perhaps you'd come to apologise.'

'Apologise?' Selwyn repeated. 'Oh, you mean for that little fiasco last night.' He laughed, clearly not in the least embarrassed. 'Yes, it was a little ludicrous, wasn't it? I can only blame the wine we had for dinner—it rather went to our heads, didn't it? Never mind, little one, next time we'll make sure that we aren't interrupted.' He moved a little closer. 'It's been quite a bonus finding you around, Linzi. Pretty girls aren't all that thick on the ground in this neck of the woods. . . .'

'Look, you seem to have the wrong idea about me, Selwyn,' said Linzi, moving away. 'I'm already engaged, and getting married in a couple of months. I'm not interested in petting sessions with you or anyone else. Sorry, but that's the way it is.'

'Oh, it is, is it?' Startled, she looked up and caught an expression of malevolence on Selwyn's face. 'That's not what I heard! Quite the reverse, in fact. I got the distinct impression that you were only too ready for the occasional bit of fun.'

Linzi stared at him, her flesh prickling with repugnance. 'What—what are you talking about?'

'Little sessions in the old chapel?' Selwyn suggested, keeping his eyes fixed on her. 'Or were you just examining the fixtures and fittings?' His smile widened foxily, showing his white teeth. 'Come off it, Linzi. You're not the pure and innocent maiden you're making yourself out to be.'

'Ceri,' Linzi said slowly. 'Ceri told you about the chapel, didn't she? Was it her idea that you should make a pass at me too? So that I could look foolish in front of Jason?'

Selwyn chuckled. 'What a vivid imagination you have! As if I need my sister to tell me what to do with a beautiful woman. And as I told you, I'll make sure there's no chance of interruption next time.' He reached out and stroked Linzi's arm with his finger. 'Change your mind, Linzi. Come out with me tonight.'

'No, thank you,' Linzi answered steadily, and moved away from his reach. 'I've told you, I'm not interested.'

'Rather stay in with Jason, eh?' Selwyn's voice took on an ugly note. 'And in just what way is that more loyal to the City banker than coming out with me?'

'There's nothing between Jason and me——'

'No? Then you won't mind my telling your boy-friend about the chapel, will you? I'm sure he'd be interested.'

Linzi closed her eyes. Just what was Selwyn playing at? What was he hoping to achieve? If he was hoping to deflect her attention from Jason—or Jason's from her—then he really needn't bother. After last night, she'd be surprised if Jason ever spoke to her again. And her own emotions were so confused that she didn't know whether she cared or not. When she thought of going back to London, never seeing Jason again, a hard knot of misery seemed to gather in her stomach. Yet the thought of Sian could change the misery into anger and disappointment, and she felt convinced that tomorrow couldn't be too soon for her departure. Bewildered, she raised a hand to her head, and opened her eyes to find Selwyn watching her.

'Look,' she said, 'I don't know what you're after, but if all you want is to blackmail me into an affair with you, you're wasting your time. I shan't be here much longer, anyway. And I really do think that Richard is more likely to believe me than you.'

'You do?' He showed his teeth again, and Linzi felt a

quiver of fear. 'All right, Linzi, we'll leave it at that. I'm sure you know your own business best. But we're still friends, aren't we?' To her surprise, he held out his hand and smiled disarmingly. 'After all, you can't really blame me for trying, can you?'

Taken aback by his effrontery, Linzi could only stare. And then a sound at the patio door made them both swing round as Jason came into the room.

Would she ever be able to see him without thinking how handsome he was? Even in working jeans and sweater, the lines of his muscular body outlined by the dark material, Jason looked as much in command as in the formal clothes he had been wearing when she had last seen him. His face was stern, as if carved from granite, and the lines of it tightened as he looked from Linzi to Selwyn and back again.

'Sorry, I seem to be in the habit of interrupting you two.'

'You're not interrupting at all,' Linzi said quickly. 'Selwyn just looked in to say hello——'

'And invite Linzi out with me,' Selwyn cut in smoothly. 'But alas, she prefers the company of Bron Melyn. You'll have to tell me your secret some time, Jason.'

Linzi caught Jason's eyes on her, bright and sardonic. 'Oh, you must have misunderstood her,' he said deliberately. 'I'm sure Linzi must have had quite enough of my dull company. Why don't you go with him, Linzi? I'm sure you'd enjoy an evening out with Selwyn.'

Linzi gazed at him in helpless fury. Was this a conspiracy or something? Last night he'd been angry because he'd found her apparently enjoying a tumble with Selwyn on the chesterfield—now he was making it impossible for her to avoid a further encounter. Perhaps he didn't think she was serious in her refusal, and wanted to see how far she would go before giving in. For a moment she was strongly tempted to accept Selwyn's invitation on the spot.

It was Selwyn himself who saved her. With a casual shrug of the shoulders he turned away, saying, 'Oh, don't push her, Jason. I think she's got a lot of sense in refusing to come out with me until she knows me better. After all, I might be a rapist for all she—or you—might know!' He turned back and gave Linzi a friendly grin. 'But you wouldn't refuse a walk on the hills during broad daylight, would you? Bring Bracken along, if it gives you any comfort—I'm sure he'd defend your honour.' And, as Linzi hesitated, he added softly: 'It might be quite interesting for you, actually. I've got some pictures you might like to see. You could give me your opinion of them.' He waited for a moment. 'Shall we say just after two? I'll come over and we'll walk up from here, shall we? And don't worry about the weather—the clouds are disappearing already.'

Linzi could find nothing to say. Her heart was hammering against her ribs. But her lack of response didn't seem to worry Selwyn. He grinned at Jason and slid out through the patio door, whistling. A few minutes later they heard his car start up and disappear down the lane.

Jason eyed Linzi speculatively.

'Well, that invitation didn't appear to fill you with joy,' he remarked. 'You look as if you've seen a ghost. I thought you liked our Selwyn?'

'You think a lot of things,' Linzi said shortly. 'Jason, you made it almost impossible for me to refuse to go out with Selwyn—why?'

'Why?' He raised one eyebrow at her. 'I don't know what you're talking about. Surely you *wanted* to go? A night out with a good-looking young man like Selwyn— why, half the girls in South Wales would jump at the chance——'

'Well, I happen to belong to the other half.' Restlessly, Linzi moved around the room. 'Look, you got the wrong idea last night—I *wasn't* enjoying a roll on the sofa with Selwyn, whatever it may have looked like. He made a pass at me, and I didn't like it——'

'Oh, I could see that!' Jason interrupted with heavy sarcasm.

'Jason, it's *true*! He took me by surprise, that's all. I was extremely relieved when you and Ceri came in——'

'Let's give it a rest, Linzi, shall we?' Jason sounded bored now as he moved to stare out of the window. 'Okay, I've got the message, you hate the sight of Selwyn, that's why you're going walking on the hills with him this afternoon. All right, I believe you.'

'I'm taking Bracken——'

'And just what protection do you think *he'll* be? He's police-trained, yes, but to hunt down criminals, not guard a maiden's chastity! I didn't notice him defending your honour up in the chapel, did you? No, he simply lay down in a corner and went to sleep.'

'I suppose he's been trained to do that too!' Linzi flashed. 'Since *you* had him, of course!'

Jason sighed. 'Here we go again. You simply won't believe I'm not the seducer of the valleys, will you?'

Jason turned away and stared out of the huge window. Higher up the valley, the clouds were already lifting, shreds of blue sky showing between them. His back was broad, stretching the fabric of his sweater, the strength of his muscles apparent in every movement. Linzi watched him, a feeling of deep despair growing in her stomach, flooding her body and limbs. She knew now that the love she felt for Jason was real, true and everlasting. Nothing could destroy it. And she longed for him to turn round, gather her into his arms and take full possession of her, ease the yearning she felt in every cell of her trembling body, and bring her the fulfilment only he could bring.

Slowly, she saw him turn back, and her heart thundered, pulsing the blood through her body so that she tingled. But he didn't move to touch her, and she knew that her moment of desire was once more to pass unassuaged. Knew too that Jason mustn't suspect her feelings, must never know how she longed to be in his arms.

She raised her chin and met his eyes with the defiance that was her only weapon.

'You'd be wiser to treat Selwyn with more caution,' Jason warned her, his face grave. 'Linzi, do you have to go out with him this afternoon? I know I made it awkward for you, but—well, I'd be happier if you rang him and called it off.'

Linzi watched him warily. His sudden change had thrown her off balance and once again she wanted to drop all her defences and run to his arms, blurt out all her worries and let him lift the burden from her. But it was too soon, too sudden. Until seconds ago, they had been fighting. How could she trust this about-face?

Jason took a step nearer and lifted her chin with one finger so that she was forced to meet his eyes. Their blue was as intense as the sea she remembered off the Cornish coast years ago. They searched her own, questioning, seeking, but she did not understand the questions he was asking—or maybe she was afraid to.

'Look, Linzi,' he said, and his voice was urgent, 'we've got to stop all this scrapping. It's not getting us anywhere. Okay, I'm as much in the wrong as you are—but you get my goat so much at times that I—oh hell, let's forget that. I just want to be sure you know what you're doing. There's this Richard—are you really sure he's the right one for you? And Selwyn—what the hell are you playing at there? I thought I knew you, Linzi—oh, I realised you'd have changed, grown up, matured—but there are changes I didn't expect, changes I don't understand and don't like. I know you don't like me to say this, Linzi, but I do still feel responsible for you. I don't want you to get hurt.'

Linzi found herself blinking away tears. He felt responsible for her—but he didn't love her. And how desperately, how achingly she needed to hear him say that. To know that he loved her as she loved him, in spite of Sian, in spite of everything that had happened between

them. But it was no use. There could never be love between them, not love of that kind. To Jason she still was,
as she would always be, his responsibility. And for her,
that simply wasn't enough.

His lips were close to hers as he whispered: 'Don't meet
Selwyn this afternoon, Linzi.'

She longed to tell him that she wouldn't. A walk with
Selwyn was the last thing she desired, especially when
there was a chance of repairing her relationship with
Jason. But Selwyn's words came back to her as she hesitated. They'd seemed almost to constitute a threat—could
well *be* a threat. And with a jolt of panic, she knew that
she would have to go.

Abruptly she turned away from Jason, leaving him
staring after her as she moved quickly across the room.

'I have to go,' she said. 'I—I've promised to go. You're
right, Jason, I don't like it when you say you still feel
responsible. It seems to me that you're doing just what
you did five years ago—using it as an excuse to keep
chains on me. Well, I'm grown up now and it won't work.'
She turned to face him, knowing that her only salvation
lay in making him angry, for she was totally unable to
stand out against his tenderness. 'I choose my own friends
now, Jason. I've been doing that quite successfully for five
years, and I think I can look after myself pretty well
without your grandfatherly advice. And since you made
it so difficult for me to refuse to go with Selwyn, I mean
to stick by my arrangements. Who knows, I might even
enjoy it. *You* seem to think I might anyway!'

Jason's face darkened. He stared at her, his eyes taking
in every detail of her appearance, the thin sweater outlining her full breasts, the jeans that hugged her small
rounded hips. Then he said shortly: 'I wish you well then,
Linzi, for there's nothing more *I* can do. But I hope to
God you know just what *you're* doing—and what you want
out of life. Because I'm damned sure I don't!'

*

The heavy clouds of the morning had, as Selwyn had forecast, dispersed by the time Linzi set off with him up the lane, but the afternoon was heavy, the heat sultry. The freshness of the past week had gone and Linzi felt hot and disinclined to climb far up the hill. Even Bracken seemed to feel it; instead of lolloping along ahead of them, he walked beside her, his tongue already hanging out.

Selwyn seemed to be completely without embarrassment as he chatted to her about his travels. He had been to Europe as well as America, she found; he dealt with all kinds of commodities, whatever was most in demand. Just now he was particularly interested in Citizens' Band radio. He had made several useful contacts in America, and had only been waiting for the legalisation date to be announced in Britain to begin selling here. You couldn't help but make money, he assured her, if you had the right eye for profit and chance.

'And you have?' Linzi said drily.

'Sure thing.' The Americanisms were back again. He glanced at her. 'Okay, Linzi, you don't have to say it. I know what you're thinking. . . . But look at it my way. You know the situation at home. Dad can't do much now. Ceri—well, she could make the big time, but I doubt it. She's not really cut out for a top-line actress. Too much hard work! And someone has to keep the Court going. There've been Penrhyses at the Court for three hundred years, did you know that? Dad and his father let a lot of the land go, but they hung on to the house. And we mean to do the same. And that takes money.'

'I see.' Linzi decided to match his frankness with some of her own. 'And that's why Ceri wants Jason, isn't it? To help with the expenses.'

'Among other things, yes,' he grinned. 'Do you blame her?'

Linzi shrugged. 'It isn't for me to blame or not.' They were out on the open moorland now. 'But I don't see where I come into it.' She met Selwyn's eyes squarely.

'Because that's why you're here now, isn't it? Do you think you need to warn me off, or something? Now that the big seduction scene's failed?'

Selwyn grinned unrepentantly. 'Something like that, yes. Ceri's really quite worried about you, Linzi, and I don't like that. Because we're very close, my sister and I. I like to see her get what she wants, especially when it's what I want her to have. We both want her to have Jason. And we don't intend to let you interfere with that.'

Linzi stopped and looked at him helplessly. 'But I'm *not* interfering! I'm Jason's model, that's all. I'll be going back to London in a week or two, perhaps even less. Ceri doesn't have a thing to worry about.' If only she did, her anguished heart exclaimed.

'Oh, give over, Linzi,' Selwyn retorted, sounding bored. 'I don't know who you're trying to kid, but no one's fooled. Anyone with half an eye can see that you two are head-over-heels about each other.'

'*What?*'

'You heard. If you're trying to keep it to yourselves for some reason, you're making a pretty poor job of it. Now, let's quit beating about the bush, Linzi. You're right, I didn't bring you up here to admire the pretty heather, and I'm not so thick I'm going to make another pass at you—not right now, anyway, though I might well have another go later on for my own amusement.... No, I want to put something to you. A business proposition.'

'A—a business proposition?' The unease that had niggled at Linzi ever since she first heard about Selwyn came back to her. She felt again the prickle of fear she had felt this morning when he had suggested the walk. She stopped and Bracken, with a sigh, flopped down on the short grass at the side of the track.

'That's a good idea,' said Selwyn. 'We'll discuss this in comfort, shall we?' He chose a flat rock and patted it, inviting Linzi to sit beside him. 'Come on, I want you to look at something.'

Slowly, like a rabbit fascinated by a snake, Linzi sat beside him. She watched as he drew a packet from his coat pocket, her muscles tensed as he unwrapped it. And as its contents came into view she let out a long, pent-up breath. It was what she had been subconsciously dreading ever since his invitation this morning.

'You've seen it before, I see,' Selwyn said softly, and held it out; a particularly lurid American 'girlie' magazine, its pages gaudy with explicit and, to Linzi's mind, obscene photographs. Idly, he riffled through the pages, turning over picture after picture of girls in various poses, pictures that sickened Linzi; until he came to the centre page. And then he spread it open on his knee and looked at it with some attention.

'All right,' Linzi whispered. It was what she'd feared ever since she had left New York. It was *why* she had left New York—the shame, the disillusionment, the reason she had wanted to give up modelling. The whole degrading, sickening business. She had begun to hope that she had successfully left it all behind her—but here it was, rearing its ugly head to torment her and spoil her life all over again. 'All right, I suppose you won't believe me if I tell you those pictures were faked?'

Selwyn shook his head cheerfully. 'Wouldn't suit my book, would it? I don't imagine you can prove it, anyway.'

Linzi shrugged. 'If I could, I'd have taken the photographer to court. *And* the magazine. Don't think I didn't try. But they were just too smart for me.'

'They sure were.' Selwyn regarded the pictures almost with affection. 'Quite a scoop for that magazine, wasn't it? The pure Linzi Berwick. . . . You must have been thankful the story never got around over here.'

'Yes, I——' Linzi realised with a kick of terror what he was driving at. 'Selwyn, you *wouldn't*——'

'Wouldn't I?' he looked thoughtful. 'Now, I wouldn't be too sure of that. I just might, you know. Starting with the boy-friend, perhaps. . . . And if that did no good, your agent—and Jason himself, of course. . . . But I don't really think any of that's going to be necessary is it, Linzi. You're going to co-operate . . . aren't you?'

Linzi bowed her head. She knew that she had no choice. Jason—and Richard—must never—*never*—see these pictures. Even though they were faked, it was so cleverly done that she herself could not have said for certain where the face, the hands and ankles that were so recognisably hers merged with the body of the more compliant model. Nobody could be blamed for thinking that it was she who had posed with such abandon.

She remembered the horror of that time in New York when she had first seen the pictures, the sickening despair that had seized her. It had all been so innocent, too—at least on her side. A few poses for a charming young photographer, nothing out of the way, not a hint of anything wrong—and then this, bursting on her with all the unpleasantness of a bombshell. It was as if a cosy household cat had suddenly turned rabid.

And now the nightmare had followed her to England. With her career beginning again, with Richard's proposal and the security promised by marriage, she had thought herself safe at last. She had begun to put behind her the fear of someone seeing those photographs and recognising—or believing they had recognised—her. But it wasn't to be. Looking up into the smiling, ruthless face of the man beside her, she knew that her fears were to prove all too real.

'What do you want me to do?' she muttered, her voice dull.

'Well, what do you think? Just get out of our way, that's all. Remove yourself, Linzi my dear. Take yourself back to London, marry your nice dull banker, live happily ever after. It's not really a lot to ask, is it?'

Not a lot? To run out on Jason for the second time? To leave him in the lurch once again? To ensure that, this time, their relationship would be destroyed for ever, with no hope of repair? The tears came to her eyes as she recalled his gentleness that morning, his kisses only a few days ago. There had been strain between them since, but might that not have been mended? And now—now there was no hope. No hope at all. For she knew that she had no choice.

'You hold all the cards, don't you?' she said dully. 'You know I'll have to go.'

'That's the general idea,' he agreed. 'If you want to keep that pure, virginal image of yours unsullied. It's up to you, Linzi dear.'

'And what about Jason? His work—he needs me for that.'

'Now, you don't really believe that, do you?' he asked. 'You know as well as I do it's just an excuse. Jason can manage perfectly well without you now, Linzi. He's done the master, hasn't he?'

'He wants me to pose in a robe, a caftan,' Linzi began, but Selwyn shook his head.

'Not necessary. Jason's a good enough sculptor to add a few flowing draperies where required. Quite frankly, I'd be surprised if he did. I had a quick glance through the studio window this morning—and I think it'd be a crying shame to hide that pretty figure.' His eyes went down to the magazine still open on his knee. 'And it seems I'm not the only one to think so.'

The sick fear in Linzi's heart was replaced by a sudden surge of fury. The worst had happened—the one thing she had dreaded above all others—and there was nothing left for her but humiliation. But she still had a right to be angry, and the emotion swept through her like a cleansing draught of fresh air in a smoky room.

With a quick movement she grabbed the magazine and ripped it apart. The pages, torn into shreds, fluttered from her hands and fell among the heather, but she couldn't leave them there to pollute the mountainside. With shaking fingers she gathered them all up and stuffed them into her rucksack.

Selwyn laughed, a note of genuine amusement in his voice as he said. 'That won't do you much good, Linzi. Think it's the only copy?'

'No, I don't think that. I just wanted to show you what I thought of your—your filthy pictures *and* your filthy proposition. All right, Selwyn, you've won. I'll go back to London and leave the field clear for your precious sister. But you needn't think you've beaten me entirely. I can still think—and I can still see you for the dirty, conniving little rat you are.' She glanced around at the rolling hillsides, the royal colours of the heather and the gorse. 'You don't deserve all this beauty, Selwyn Penrhys. You say you love it—or I suppose that's why you want to keep it—but I don't understand how you can, and still act the way you do. But there's nothing I can do about it. I can only go, and hope that by going I'll have prevented at least some of the corruption, some of the rot you've brought here.' She stood up and looked down at the handsome man at her feet. 'Don't bother to come any further, Selwyn. I'd rather finish my walk on my own, or just with Bracken—he's better company.'

Selwyn didn't follow her as she went on up the track, bitterly aware that this could be the last time she would walk here. But the sour taste the encounter had left remained in her mouth, and she knew that it would be a long time before she recovered from the unpleasantness of his threats.

By the time Linzi returned from her walk she had, to some extent, come to terms with the fact that she must leave Bron Melyn. Her unhappiness had grown with the knowledge that this time there would be no return. The feeling she had discovered in herself, the love she had for Jason, must remain for ever in her heart, a secret that even he would never know. She would have to go away,

knowing that she was unlikely ever to see him again,
knowing that this time he must surely hate her for her
apparent double rejection of him. Knowing that there was
nothing left for her but a safe, dull marriage with
Richard. . . .

But was there even that? Could she marry Richard now,
knowing that she didn't love him—had never really loved
him? He had never represented more than an escape, she
realised, a way of life that would take her out of the stresses
of modelling and give her security, a home and family.
Could she still take it, after these stormy weeks with Jason?
Did she even *want* to?

She recognised that Richard's love for her hadn't been
any more passionate. He had been quite objective about
it, she saw now, and quite honest. He too had wanted a
home and family, the kind of background a man in his
position might be expected to have. A beautiful wife to be
his hostess, to entertain, to be at his side when he attended
social functions. Love, as Linzi knew it, hadn't entered
his calculations simply because they *were* calculations.
Perhaps he had never actually experienced it.

She wouldn't be cheating Richard if she married him,
knowing that she didn't love him. She would be able to
give him what he wanted. They might even have a
reasonably happy life together. But wouldn't she be
cheating herself?

Yet—if she *didn't* marry him—then a home and family
would never be hers. Because no other man would ever
be able to offer her more than Richard did. No other
man could ever replace Jason.

The house was empty when Linzi at last let herself in.
She wandered slowly through the rooms, noticing again
the conversions that Jason had made in the old farmhouse;
the comfort, the good taste. She could be happy here. . . .
But that dream was over, if it had ever existed. It was
Ceri who would live here with Jason. Ceri, with whom he
was at least half in love; Ceri, who was determined and

pretty and used to having her own way, and likely to get it yet again. Unless, of course, they went to live at Penrhys Court. But before that happened, Linzi would be gone— gone and forgotten.

In her bedroom, she looked helplessly round, not sure just where to start. She knew that Selwyn's threats had not been empty ones—he meant her to leave Bron Melyn, and the sooner the better. Now, with the house empty, had to be the ideal time. But unhappiness had brought a heaviness to Linzi's limbs, a reluctance to start the packing that meant the end of everything for her.

Well, it was no use putting it off. Unpleasant jobs were always best tackled at once. With grim determination, Linzi lifted her suitcases down from the top of a wardrobe. Hardly caring about creases, she began to empty the wardrobe of clothes and stuff them in. . . .

The room looked denuded when she had finished. Only a few tissues in the waste-paper basket, the crumpled bedclothes and a used towel in the bathroom showed that she had been here. She stood looking round, suddenly despondent. It wouldn't be long now. But after the walk on the hill in the humid heat and the flurry of packing, she felt hot and sticky. She would have a shower before she left. Even Selwyn wouldn't begrudge her that.

The tepid spray refreshed her and she stayed under it, letting it soak her hair and wishing that her worries could be washed away as easily as the stickiness of her body. Misery invaded her. If only she'd never come here! She would never have known her true feelings for Jason, never have had to face the humiliation from Selwyn, never have had to question her feelings for Richard. She should have taken his advice in the beginning, she reflected bitterly. He had been right to have doubts. And she wondered again just why Jason had brought her here. Was it just for the sculpture—or did he have some other reason?

Well, there was little use in speculating now. Deciding

that she had been in the shower long enough, Linzi stepped out and wrapped herself in a large, fluffy bath towel before wandering back into her bedroom.

And saw Jason Carver, his huge muscular body rigid with anger, standing in the doorway.

Linzi swallowed and stepped back involuntarily. But before she could escape into the bathroom, Jason had made one stride to cross the room and had her in his grasp. Trembling, she looked up at him, her topaz eyes wide with panic. But his gaze was hostile, the lines of his face harsh, his mouth set in a grim, hard line, and she knew that there was to be no pleading with him this time.

'And just what's going on now, Linzi?' he grated. 'Running out on me again, are you? You make quite a habit of it, don't you? Only this time you're not going to get away with it so easily. You're going to stay here and face up to me and tell me just why you find me so repugnant!'

Linzi quivered between his hands. Why had she taken that shower? she asked herself despairingly. She could have been out of here by now, heading back towards London, the whole unhappy business behind her. Now what was she to do?

'I'm waiting for an answer,' Jason growled, and his hands tightened on her wet, bare shoulders.

She bit her lip. She was acutely aware of the towel that was her only covering. Jason drew her closer and she felt the heat radiating from his body, through the thin cream shirt he wore. As her breast touched the wall of his chest she was conscious of the strong beating of his heart, and her head swam.

'Jason, I can't explain,' she whispered. 'Let me go, please. It—it's better this way.'

'You expect me to accept that?' The harshness in his voice was terrifying and Linzi squirmed against him in her efforts to escape. Her movements brought a quickening of his breath, and he held her hard against his body, one hand forcing her head back so that she had to meet his eyes. 'Linzi, tell me the truth. What's got into you? Why have you decided to go?'

'Don't pretend you want me here!' she flashed. 'We've done nothing but fight ever since I arrived. You've never forgiven me for that first time, have you? That's why you brought me here—so that you could torment me, so that you could play with my feelings like a cat plays with a mouse, letting me go a little way, then dragging me back again—you don't want me yourself, Jason, but you don't want anyone else to have me. Not Selwyn, or Richard, or *anyone*! Let me go,' she sobbed, the tears pouring down her cheeks. 'Please, *please* let me go!'

'Why should I?' His hands were cruelly tight on her shoulders. 'Tell me that! Why *should* I let you go, let someone else have you, someone who just happens along and takes your fancy? Haven't I waited for years? Didn't I have to wait for you to grow up? Wasn't it enough that you threw me over five years ago, for no good reason, and I've had to wait patiently ever since? Well, my patience doesn't last for ever, Linzi, and now I——'

'There *was* a good reason,' she interrupted frantically, aware that it was now only the pressure of his body against hers that kept the towel in place. 'I *had* to go, Jason, don't you understand? We were getting married for the wrong reasons—because you wanted to take care of me, yes, because you'd made a promise—because I had a schoolgirl crush on you. But not because we *loved* each other—not as adults should love. Don't you see that? Don't you know that's true?'

Brilliant blue eyes stared into hers. A strong, square hand slid up her back, moving slowly over the warm, damp skin to lift the tangle of wet chestnut hair away from her neck, fingers winding themselves around in it. A change came into the expression on the ravaged face, a tenderness that smoothed out the harsh lines and softened the diamond-hardness of the eyes. With his other hand,

Jason touched her cheek, letting his fingers trace the outline of her face, and the fire from his fingertips ran down her neck and into her body, so that she quivered again—not with fear this time, but with a warm rush of desire that left her giddy.

'So we didn't love as adults should love?' he murmured. 'Well, maybe you're right there—though *I* was adult enough. But now we're *both* grown-up, aren't we? Grown-up enough to put an end to this crazy warring between us, adult enough to admit what's really going on.' His lips came close to hers as he whispered: 'I want you, Linzi, and you want me. We've been this way ever since the moment you first walked into the house—don't let's deny it. We've lost five years—we can't afford to lose any more. Linzi. . . .' With a swift movement he whipped the towel away and flung it aside, leaving her naked. 'Don't let's waste any more time.'

Linzi closed her eyes as he lifted her from her feet and carried her over to the bed. This time, his movements were gentleness itself as he lifted the covers and laid her on the sheet. But he didn't cover her again. Instead he stood looking down at her, and Linzi opened her eyes to see reverence on his face as well as desire.

'You're beautiful, Linzi,' he muttered thickly, and he ran one hand with exquisite tenderness down the length of her body. 'There's not one part of you that isn't beautiful—perfect. Linzi, I've dreamed about this moment. It's kept me awake at nights, the thought of you in my arms at last, warm and willing, ready to be mine. Sometimes I thought the time would never come—but it has, Linzi my darling, hasn't it? *Hasn't it?*'

His last words were an urgent whisper against her mouth. Linzi felt his fingers making their exploration of her body; tracing a line of flame from the hollow of her throat, circling her breasts, teasing the nipples into erection; curving over her stomach and the soft warmth of her thighs. Her mind reeled, her thoughts fused in a bewildering whirlpool of excitement. Her arms snaked up round his neck, dragging his mouth hard against hers, and as they drank deeply of each other's kisses, she let one hand slip forward to unbutton his shirt. With a thrill of delight she felt his skin touch hers, and then he was fumbling at his waistband, drawing away from her to slide out of his own clothes . . . and coming back to claim her, stretching the full length of his massive body against hers, moving against her in a way that had her whimpering for fulfilment.

'Not yet, my sweet,' he murmured raggedly, his fingers playing upon her body as a violinist plays upon his instrument, turning her to an exquisite rapture before letting her attain the final crescendo. 'Not yet. We've a lot of time behind us, a lot of catching up to do . . . and all the time in the world in which to enjoy doing it.' His mouth found hers again, gentle yet possessive, his lips manipulating hers to fresh joy. Linzi let her body move against his, delighting in the smoothness of her skin against his rough maleness. Tentatively at first, then more boldly, she let her hands make their own journey, pressing against the hardness of his ribs, the flat stomach, the taut skin of his thighs. Sinuously, he shifted closer still, gathering her against him, enfolding her in himself so that they lay twined together, moving gently in unison, a tangle of warm passionate human flesh.

'You know something?' Jason murmured as his lips found the lobe of her ear and played with it. 'I'm never letting you go again. This time you stay—and you stay for good. Nothing's going to come between us this time, Linzi, but *nothing*.' His arms tightened and Linzi gasped for breath. 'There just isn't room!'

And then, even as he shifted his position for the last, final assault of ecstasy; even as his body snaked over hers, his knee driving between her thighs, Linzi saw again the pictures in the American magazine. The pictures Selwyn had gloated over. The pictures that, if Jason ever saw them, would fill him with a horror and repugnance even deeper than hers, too deep for him ever to understand or believe her innocence.

She couldn't let it happen. But if she let this situation continue, if she let Jason possess her now, so that she was utterly committed to him—happen it would. And the hurt it must cause him would be more searing than any simple rejection.

There was no more time to lose. In seconds it would be too late, for she knew that once Jason had made love to her fully, there would be no going back. With a strength that astonished her, she twisted violently, tipping Jason off balance. With a gasp of surprise, he fell back at her side and Linzi rolled rapidly away from him, off the side of the bed, and scrambled for her clothes. She was already into her jeans, struggling to fasten the zip, when Jason recovered and jerked himself from the bed, his face bewildered and angry, his eyes snapping fire.

'What the hell did you do that for? What are you playing at now? *Linzi!*' He reached out, but for once Linzi was too quick for him. She twisted out of his grasp, pulling her shirt round her as she did so. Dressed, she felt at a distinct advantage. She let her eyes run over Jason's body, though it stabbed her to do so, and said cuttingly:

'It's no use, Jason—you're just not quite persuasive enough. Almost—but not quite.' She dropped her eyes from the expression in his and said wearily. 'I'm sorry. I meant to be gone before you came back. Now—please—will you let me go?'

'*Let* you go?' Jason snarled, his face contorted now with fury. 'After that, little Linzi, I'll be only too pleased to *help* you go. My God, but you're a real prize-winning tease, aren't you?' He came closer and Linzi cringed. 'One of these days you're going to get yourself hurt, you little fool, don't you realise that? And when it happens, don't ask *me* to pick up the pieces—I'll be only too glad to help shovel them into the bin, along with the rest of the rubbish!'

He wrenched himself away and grabbed his clothes. Linzi watched dumbly as he stormed out of the room with them, retaining in his magnificent nakedness a dignity that she envied. She heard the door to his bedroom slam, and then there was silence.

Slowly she picked up her cases and carried them down the oak staircase. Slowly she packed the car. She took a long look around at Bron Melyn, at the flower-tubs outside the door, at the long grey studio, at the golden hills that rose above the house and the dark purple line of the mountains beyond. Then she got into the Mini and drove carefully out into the lane.

When she reached a quiet spot where she could safely pull in, she stopped the car, put her head down on the steering wheel, and cried as though her heart would break.

CHAPTER EIGHT

THE sound of heavy rain woke Linzi from an uneasy sleep, and she turned her head towards the greyness of the window in an attempt to judge the time.

It was light, so morning must have come. Not that it mattered a lot, although she was always thankful when the long night was over. It was during the small hours that she felt the worst. At two or three o'clock in the morning, when even the traffic was stilled and all London slept. When it seemed that she must be the only person in the world awake, totally alone in her unhappiness. She would lie there then, staring into the darkness, reliving every moment of the past few weeks, imagining life at Bron Melyn going on without her. Jason, completing his sculpture—would he really be able to finish it without her, as Selwyn had said? And Selwyn, smiling his foxy smile as Ceri continued with her plans and eventually, as Linzi was quite sure she would, succeeding in them to become Jason's wife and mistress of Bron Melyn.

Her thoughts would become too much for her then, and as often as not Linzi would swing abruptly from the bed and snap on the light to go to her little kitchen and make a hot drink. She must have drunk enough milk to bathe Cleopatra in, she reflected ruefully, stirring yet another cup of chocolate. It was probably all that helped her survive anyway, for during the day her appetite was minimal.

This morning it seemed that the fine weather had really broken at last. It had been threatening for some days— sometimes fine, sometimes showery, and with one or two quite violent thunderstorms. Wearily, her eyes and head heavy, Linzi got up and drew the curtains to look out at the wet street. Rain streamed down the roofs around her, splashing into the puddles below. A few bedraggled starlings perched along the guttering and a small dog, its coat plastered to its sides, trotted along the opposite pavement. Otherwise there was no sign of life.

A wet Sunday in London, Linzi thought wryly. Empty streets, empty parks, empty everything. Symbols of an empty life—the life hers had become. And, although she had told herself again and again that it did no good, she let her thoughts drift back again to Bron Melyn.

What would a wet Sunday be like there? She had known Bron Melyn only in sunshine. She imagined Hugh bringing in logs and piling them in the big stone fireplace in the sitting-room, setting them ablaze. Jason, no doubt, would go over to the studio to do some work. Perhaps later, he would take Bracken up on the hills and they would both come back soaked to towel themselves dry and stretch out before Hugh's log fire. And then there would be dinner, with the heavy curtains drawn to shut out the weather, and the room filled with flickering fire-glow, and the strains of music from Jason's stereo.

Suddenly her flat, although warmed by central heating and furnished with care over the years, seemed cold and bare. It wasn't home any more, Linzi thought, looking round with critical eyes. The walls were too smooth, the furniture too modern. There had been no real *life* here; no loving, no noise of children, no family laughter and tears. The atmosphere that took generations to build up was missing, and probably would never exist between the stark walls of these too-square, over-convenient little rooms.

A bitter longing filled her heart. A longing for the old farmhouse that looked as if it had grown in the mountains; a longing for the mountains themselves, with their long ridges, their table-tops, their jagged rocks and steep valleys, their gay little rivers and profusion of colour. And, above all, a longing for the man who lived at Bron Melyn. The man who looked as if he himself had been carved from the granite, with his rugged profile and craggy face. The man who had had possession of her heart ever since she was a child; whose single glance from brilliant sapphire eyes could turn her bones to water, her flesh to fire and her mind to oblivion.

Restlessly, Linzi turned away from the window and its dreary outlook, and went into the kitchen. With a listlessness that was fast becoming habit, she made coffee and drank half of it, poured milk on a bowl of cornflakes and ate only two or three spoonfuls. She switched on the radio but scarcely heard the music that poured from it, and when the music stopped and a Sunday service began she snapped it off irritably. Making her bed seemed almost too great an effort, and a shower and fresh clothes only made her feel marginally better.

She was drinking another cup of coffee and staring indifferently at the Sunday paper when someone knocked on the door. Linzi's heart jumped. She laid down the paper and looked towards the door with frightened eyes, willing whoever it was to go away. But the knocking persisted, and after a moment or two she heard a voice calling her name.

'Linzi! Linzi, are you there? *Linzi!*'

'*Richard!*' she breathed, and shrank back in her chair. What was Richard doing here? He was supposed to be abroad—why had he come here, to her flat?

She kept silent, hoping he would go away, but he continued to knock and call. And at last, his voice exasperated and edged with something else—surely not fear?—he shouted: 'Linzi, this is your last chance! If you're there, open the door and let me in. Or I'll go and fetch the porter and get *him* to let me in! Now, what's it to be?'

With a heavy sigh, Linzi swung to her feet and crossed the room. She unlocked the door and pulled it back.

Richard, wearing a dripping mackintosh, his face red and angry, stared at her.

'So you *were* in there!' he exclaimed. 'I thought you would be—Linzi, what in God's name are you playing at? What's all this hiding in aid of? Do you realise that nobody has known where you were for the past week?'

'Well, that's their hard luck,' Linzi retorted, adding wearily, 'Oh, don't stand there, Richard. You'd better come in.'

He followed her into the living-room, looking critically around him. Linzi shrugged and flopped back into her armchair. She knew the place looked neglected, she just hadn't had the energy to dust or tidy up, any more than she had had the energy to cook meals or put on make-up. She brushed her hair back from her pale face and looked up at Richard. Had he got fatter since he had been away, she wondered without any real interest, or had his stocky build been running to plumpness before that?

Richard stood on the hearthrug, his hands behind his back, and looked down at her censoriously. 'Well? I'm waiting for an explanation, Linzi.'

His assuming attitude lit a small flare of annoyance. 'I wasn't aware that I owed you any,' she retorted sharply.

'Not aware that you owed me an explanation? Linzi, do you realise that I cut short an important business trip because I was worried about you? Do you realise that I flew to Cardiff, hired a car to take me to that benighted place at the back of nowhere that your ex-employer is pleased to call his *studio*—only to find that you'd vanished, left him for some reason he either didn't know or didn't care to explain, and taken off for God knows where. Even Anna didn't know where you were. I came here just as a last chance, in case you might have left some clue at least as to where you might be. I've been telephoning at every opportunity—where have you been that you didn't hear it?'

'I did hear it,' Linzi confessed indifferently. 'I covered it up with pillows.'

'You—you *covered it up with pillows*?' Richard's face was suffused with scarlet. 'Linzi, have you gone out of your mind?'

'Perhaps,' she acknowledged. 'Have you driven up from Wales this morning, Richard? You must have started out in the middle of the night. Would you like some coffee?' She made her remarks automatically, not really caring whether he had coffee or not. But he nodded and sat down suddenly in the other armchair, and she realised with a faint pang that he really was exhausted. Poor Richard, she thought as she went to make the coffee. He wasn't having much luck.

When she returned, he had calmed down a little and was sitting with his head back and eyes closed. She stood looking down at him, wondering idly why she had ever even considered spending the rest of her life in his company. He would have driven her mad within weeks, she thought, comparing his thinning hair with Jason's thick black thatch, his pale, pudgy face with Jason's strong profile, stamped with his powerful personality. And that short, almost tubby body! The memory of Jason's iron arms, holding her close against his broad, muscular frame, shook her for a moment. She handed Richard his coffee and returned to her chair.

The silence stretched between them. Linzi thought that perhaps she ought to make an effort, ask him why he had interrupted his tour and gone to Wales, but she just didn't have the energy. She wasn't being fair, she knew that, but somehow what Richard did had ceased to have any interest for her. She just wished he would drink his coffee and go away, leaving her with her thoughts.

But Richard evidently had no intention of doing that. At last, with obvious irritation, he demanded: 'Well? Aren't you going to say *anything*?'

Linzi roused herself. 'What do you want me to say?'

He gestured helplessly. 'Tell me why you left Wales,

for a start. Why you didn't let anyone know where you were. Why you haven't been answering your phone.' He leaned forward. 'Linzi, I've been worried out of my mind about you!'

Linzi looked at him. He really did look upset. With a pang of remorse, she said gently, 'Yes, I'm sorry, Richard. I can see I should have let you know I'd left. But I'd no idea you were going to come looking for me, had I? So far as I knew, you were somewhere between Vienna and Paris, or Madrid or wherever your next stop was. I didn't deliberately cause you worry.'

'Well, I don't suppose you did,' he said, slightly mollified. 'But it was extremely thoughtless of you, to say the least.'

Linzi bent her head. She already knew that Richard had a tendency to grumble on about things that had upset him. There was no way of stopping him, it just had to be tolerated until his hurt feelings were appeased. After a while, he said: 'Well, you still haven't told me why you left.'

Linzi shrugged. 'It just didn't work out.' No way was she going to tell Richard the truth about what had happened between her and Jason.

Richard looked complacent. 'So I was right, then.'

'I didn't say that. Look, Richard, let's leave it at that, shall we? Things didn't work out and I decided to leave and come home. I didn't get in touch with you straightaway because I wasn't sure where you'd be and I didn't want you to worry. Anyway, I just felt like being on my own for a while.'

'And that's why you didn't tell anyone, not even Anna, that you were here? Why you didn't answer your phone?'

'Yes, that's why,' Linzi agreed with a sigh.

'H'm.' Richard finished his coffee and got up to put the mug on the table. He glanced round at her, his eyes narrow in the plump flesh of his cheeks. 'Well, I'm not satisfied that you're telling me everything, Linzi, but we'll leave it there. No doubt you'll confide in me one day. In any case, I can guess what happened.' His mouth thinned with disapproval. 'Carver's obviously a barbarian—living out there at the back of beyond in that dreadful old house. Oh, he's made quite a showplace of it, I agree, but can you imagine what it must be like in winter? It was bad enough yesterday, with the rain lashing down—but once the cold weather starts, with snow and ice, it must be virtually inaccessible.' He moved across to the window and gazed complacently down at the wet London street. 'Thank God to be back in civilisation, anyway! I can understand your need to recover, Linzi. And I'm thankful that you had the sense to do as I told you and come back, even if it did cause a little confusion.'

'Let's get this straight, Richard,' Linzi roused herself to say. 'I didn't come back because you *told* me to—I came because I *chose* to.'

Richard smiled patronisingly and Linzi looked round for something to throw at him. 'No, of course you didn't. But you're here, aren't you? And I'm very pleased that you are. I'm only surprised you stayed as long as you did—as I said, Carver has some very strange notions. I saw some of his sculptures.' He wrinkled his nose fastidiously.

'And just what was the matter with them?' Linzi was beginning to feel really angry now. God, how pompous Richard was! How was it she'd never noticed it before? And how could she ever have borne to live with it?

'The matter?' He had a high, shrill laugh too, she noticed disgustedly. 'Linzi, you saw them! Why, some of them are highly suggestive. Or perhaps you're a little too naïve to have realised.'

'No, I don't think I'm naïve.' Linzi kept her temper with difficulty. 'I don't think Jason's work is suggestive, either. I think it's sensitive, beautiful and evocative—but anything suggestive about it is in your mind, Richard, not in Jason's work.'

He looked at her in surprise. 'Linzi! That's not a nice thing to say!'

'Well, I'm not feeling very nice at the moment,' she snapped. 'So if you don't like me the way I am, perhaps you'd better go.'

Richard stared at her. 'You've changed, Linzi,' he said slowly. 'Something's happened to you since I've been away. What is it? What happened at Bron Melyn? *What did that brute do to you?*'

He came towards her and Linzi recoiled as he took her arms in his plump fingers. She jerked away and moved restlessly towards the kitchen, saying wearily, 'Oh, for heaven's sake, Richard, don't be so melodramatic! Jason's not a brute, and he didn't do anything to me.' And that was an out-and-out lie, she reflected, remembering the things Jason had done to her, both physically and emotionally. But she wasn't prepared to tell Richard about them. In fact, she was tired of the entire conversation, and she looked at him, wishing he would go. But he was still standing there, watching her, his face creased with suspicion.

'Look, Richard,' she said at last, 'there really isn't any point in us continuing with this. All right, I *am* different. I've changed in my—my feelings towards you. I'm sorry, Richard, but I just don't want to go on with our engagement. It wouldn't work, I know that now.' She went towards the bedroom. 'I'll give you back your ring now.'

Richard's eyes goggled as she moved towards him. His pale face flushed, his mouth opened and closed, and he uttered a faint sound of protest. But he made no move to touch her as she went past him and through the door. And when she came out and handed him his ring, he took it and stared at it almost in disbelief.

'You—you want to break our engagement?' he spluttered at last. 'Linzi, you can't be serious. You're ill—I thought you looked off colour when I came in! Look, you mustn't do this—you must see a doctor, you're run down, probably need a tonic. It's my fault for letting you go away on that ridiculous job, with that dreadful man.' He pawed at her arm in agitation. 'Don't worry, my dear, everything will be all right. I'm sorry if I was harsh with you, but I'd been worried, you understand that, don't you? Linzi, come and sit down, Linzi——'

'Oh, stop it, *stop* it, for God's sake!' Linzi shrieked. 'You're like a hysterical old woman! Richard, I'm sorry, but I *do* mean it—I don't want to marry you, I *can't* marry you, it would never, never work, not in a million years. We don't *love* each other, can't you see that? *You* don't love *me*—you just want a hostess, a status symbol, someone to have a nice neat two point three children for you and bring them up and send them to all the right schools. I don't think you even know what love is, not real love. And I don't love you. I want—oh, I want——'

But she could go no further. The full realisation of what she wanted and could never have burst upon her and she flung herself away from Richard and into a chair, the tears torn from her body in a series of painful, wrenching sobs.

For several minutes the room was still, Linzi's sobs the only sound to break the heavy silence. Then Richard spoke, his voice flat and toneless.

'I see. Yes, I see. You haven't been entirely truthful with me, Linzi, have you? You say nothing happened, but something did. It's Carver, isn't it? You're in love with him—or imagine yourself to be. And in such circumstances, of course, I don't stand a chance.'

'Richard——'

'No, don't make it worse.' He straightened his shoulders and went back to the hearth, his back stiff. 'I can quite see that a man like Carver has more—personal magnetism—than myself. I'm not quite so blind as you seem to think me, Linzi. But I'm not at all sure that what he can offer you is any better, in the long run, than what I

offer. However, I can't expect you to understand that.'
He put the ring carefully away in his waistcoat pocket.
'I'm sorry you feel like this. I had hoped—but there it is.
I'd better go.'

'Richard,' said Linzi, raising a tear-stained face, 'you've
got it wrong. Jason isn't offering me anything. I don't
expect ever to see him again. Yes, you're right, I *do* love
him. But he doesn't love me, and he never will. I destroyed all chances of that long ago.'

'And yet you still don't want to marry me?' he asked,
and she shook her head.

'I can't.'

There was a long silence. Richard sighed, glanced out
of the window at the rain and then sat down again. He
seemed to be making up his mind to speak, and Linzi
watched him curiously. At last he shot her a glance, then
said:

'Then would you mind telling me the reason for this?'

Linzi reached out and took the scrap of paper he was
holding out. It was a flimsy, pale blue sheet—an air-letter.
It was addressed to Richard at his hotel in Vienna, and it
said:

*If you want to marry Linzi Berwick, better hurry home. There's
more than sculpting going on in that studio.*

Linzi stared at it, feeling cold and sick. She raised her
eyes at last and whispered: 'Who?'

'You tell me.' Richard lifted his shoulders. 'Not a pretty
thing to receive, was it?'

'Richard, I——' She wanted to say it wasn't true, but
the words wouldn't come. Nothing, indeed, had ever
happened in the studio—Jason had never been anything
but the professional sculptor there, totally absorbed in his
work. But in other places? In the chapel—in her bedroom? Feeling her cheeks turn scarlet, she looked down at
the paper again.

'And this is why you came back?' she asked in a low
voice.

'I didn't want to lose you,' he said simply, and she felt guilt and remorse flood her body. All right, he'd wanted her for the wrong reasons—but she still hadn't played fair with him. There had still been times when her need for Jason had almost come before her loyalty to Richard.

'I'm sorry,' she said at last. 'Richard, I really am sorry. But it doesn't make any difference, I'm afraid. I still can't marry you—even though I know I'll never be able to marry Jason.'

'Well, that seems to be that, then.' He stood up. 'Not that I think you'd be well advised to marry Carver, anyway. He struck me as a very strange man. Morose, curt—even the girl he was helping seemed half scared of him. I felt quite sorry for her, though he'd obviously been doing quite a lot for her.'

'Girl?' Linzi said absently, still staring at the letter and wondering who could have sent it. 'What girl was that?'

'Oh, some local child with an illegitimate baby—didn't look more than seventeen at the outside. Carver did tell me part of the story, since I arrived in the middle of it. All rather squalid, but what can you expect in these primitive parts? Actually, it was nothing short of feudal.' Richard shrugged into his raincoat and picked up his umbrella. 'Local landowner seduces village maiden—that kind of thing. Only in the old days they never minded taking the consequences for their bit of fun, never let the children want for anything. This one didn't want to, it seems. Your friend Carver took a hand and persuaded him that he should, and now the child's getting an adequate maintenance payment. Quite right too, though I must say I was surprised at a man like Carver taking so much trouble over it.'

He turned at the door and took her hand, but Linzi waved aside his next speech. Her brain was spinning— *local landowner—village maiden—Jason* taking a hand? What did it all mean?

'Linzi——' Richard began, but she cut him short.

'The girl? Did he tell you her name? The *local* girl,' she added impatiently. 'The girl with the baby.'

'Oh, her.' Clearly, Richard didn't understand her sudden interest. 'Oh, some Welsh name, can't remember it now. Never quite caught it, to tell you the truth. Linzi——'

'Was it—was it Sian?' She hardly dared ask, but Richard wrinkled his brow and nodded.

'Yes, that's it. Never heard it before.' He tried again. 'Linzi, don't decide too quickly about—you know, about us. You're upset now and I understand that, but I'm sure when you've thought things over you'll see things more reasonably. And when you do, don't hesitate to get in touch. I'll—well, I'll be waiting.'

Linzi looked at him and smiled. Dear Richard! He still couldn't really believe that she would turn him down. Safely ensconced in his world of money and status, he was comfortably sure that no girl with any sense could refuse his offerings of money, marriage and lifelong security. He didn't even know that nobody on earth could offer that.

Well, it would save his pride for him to go on thinking that. And by the time he realised that she wasn't going to get in touch, he would have stopped missing her and got used to leading his own life again. Perhaps some day he would meet a girl who wanted what he had to give, and could give him in return the things he wanted from a wife.

And although she couldn't be absolutely certain yet, Linzi was more than half sure that he'd given *her* something that she needed badly. For that alone, she had to be grateful.

'Goodbye, Richard,' she said softly, and leaned forward to kiss him lightly on the cheek. 'And I hope the rest of the trip goes well.'

'My goodness, yes,' he said, glancing at his watch. 'There's a flight to Paris in an hour's time—I might just make it, if I hurry!'

Linzi sighed a little as she closed the door after him. Richard would never change. Totally self-absorbed, completely self-satisfied—why had she never seen it before? But she'd had other problems then, she reminded herself. Her flight from New York after the publication of those photographs—her decision to give up modelling and the worries that had come from not knowing how she was to earn a living. And Richard had been kind and attentive. Good manners were important to him, and he would never really be anything else.

And now he was gone, and she could give her full attention to what he had told her. He'd been to Bron Melyn and met Jason! Jason had been curt and morose—what did that mean? And Sian—Richard had seen Sian, seen that Jason was helping her, had heard the story of her seduction by a local 'landowner'—surely that could only be Selwyn—and had only mentioned it casually, in passing, as he was about to leave.

Was it true? *Was* it Selwyn who had made Sian pregnant, and not Jason, after all? Had she been mistaken?

With trembling fingers, Linzi made another cup of coffee. She tried to recall every word spoken on the subject of Sian, including those by Sian herself. Who had told her Jason was the father of the dark-haired little baby? Sian hadn't. And Jason, although he'd never denied it, had never actually confirmed it either. The only person who had said straight out that Sian's baby could be Jason's— and even she hadn't actually said it *was*—was Ceri.

And Ceri wanted Jason for herself. Wanted Linzi out of the way, and had told her so.

Sipping the hot coffee, Linzi thought again of the letter Richard had received. Someone had known where to find him, someone who wanted to remove Linzi from Bron Melyn. Ceri fitted the second requirement—but what of the first?

And she remembered the night Richard had telephoned. The way he'd told her the address of his hotel in

Vienna; and the way she'd repeated it aloud as she wrote it down.

Ceri had been at Bron Melyn that night. She'd been in the living-room and the door had been ajar. She could quite easily have heard every word Linzi said.

'My God,' Linzi muttered. 'The liar! The nasty, cheating, spying little *witch*!'

Her depressed lethargy had vanished. Consumed with an angry energy, she roamed about the flat, going over the whole thing in her mind, over and over again, until she believed she had the picture clear. Ceri had feared her from the start. She had been resentful that Jason had chosen a London model for his figure instead of herself, and she'd been suspicious of his determination that it should be Linzi Berwick. As soon as she had seen Jason and Linzi together she'd sensed the undercurrents, the tension between them—and she'd guessed only too accurately what had been going on in the chapel. It wasn't surprising that she'd made up her mind to get rid of Linzi, and she'd used every trick at her disposal to do so. She must have written to Richard before Selwyn had come home—and it had been an additional bonus to her armoury to find that he not only knew of Linzi Berwick, but knew something very much to her disadvantage.

She had even manipulated Linzi into believing that Jason could be the father of a local girl's baby and was denying it—when all the time the culprit was her own brother!

Well, that was one thing she *could* put right, Linzi determined. She knew Jason well enough to realise that he must have been bitterly hurt by her accusations regarding Sian. Too hurt to deny them—his pride would have compelled him to allow her to go on believing the worst, considering that she should have had more trust. As indeed she should, Linzi admitted humbly. He deserved her apology. And not just by letter, either. This was an apology that must be delivered in person.

Her mind made up, Linzi swung into action. The flat was dusty and untidy—it wouldn't take long to put that right. For some reason, she felt she had to leave everything as neat as possible, as a symbol of a fresh start. Quickly she whisked through the apartment, making the bed, tidying the sitting-room, freshening up the bathroom and clearing the kitchen.

She hadn't even unpacked one of her suitcases when she'd arrived at the beginning of the week, she had been so depressed. Now, she threw a few more clothes into her other and lifted them both. Why, she had no idea. Jason was as likely to show her the door as to listen to her now. But hope sang in her heart and a smile quivered on her lips as she closed the door behind her and hurried down the stairs.

Though what reason she had to be optimistic, heaven only knew, she told herself wryly as she threw the cases into the back of the Mini and slid into the driving seat. Jason's welcome to her was hardly likely to be any more fulsome than Richard had found it. And her face grew grave again as she recalled that last encounter between her and Jason. A tingle ran fierily through her body as she thought of the way they had lain together on her bed, close in each other's arms, their mouths and hands and limbs taking joy in each other and promising a fulfilment that never came. Jason's pride must have taken quite a beating when she rolled away from him, off the bed, making it plain that her arousal hadn't by any means matched his—and if only he knew the truth, she thought with a groan. But he didn't, and it was too late to convince him.

Would he even care that she now knew the truth about Sian? Would he even let her into the house? Or would he send her away, and this time for ever?

Well, if he did, it would be no more than she deserved. And at least she had to try.

With her optimism gone and a grim determination in

its place, Linzi drove to the nearest garage to fill her petrol tank and check that the Mini was fit for a long drive. Then, with the windscreen-wipers switching relentlessly back and forth against the streaming rain, she turned west and headed resolutely through the storm for Wales.

CHAPTER NINE

DARKNESS was already falling when Linzi arrived at last at Crickhowell. The rain had not eased all day, and a strong wind besides had made the journey more hazardous than she liked. Several times she had felt the little car swerve as a gust of wind caught it, and the spray from other vehicles had been too much at times for the wipers. She was thankful to find the end of the journey in sight, and at the same time increasingly nervous and worried about her reception.

Now that she was almost there, Jason's possible reaction to her unannounced arrival seemed more and more uncertain. As she drove into the little town she even looked around for a hotel, half inclined to put up for the night and go back to London next day without even having seen him. But that would be stupid, she scolded herself. Stupid and cowardly. She owed Jason an apology, right? Then that was what she would do. What *he* did about it was another matter entirely. At least she would have lost nothing, and there must be the faint chance of a gain.

Rain slooshed down her windscreen as she turned into the narrow lane and drove slowly up it, thinking how different this was from the first time she had come here. Then, the lane had been bathed in blazing sunshine. Now it was dark and wet, the sullen clouds bringing a heavy gloom. The bracken that had been green and gold was now dead-looking, its bedraggled fronds catching at the sides of the Mini with slimy fingers. The rain had flattened the grass along the banks and the hedges dripped soddenly. Under the wheels of the car, the uneven surface of the road was wet and muddy, with deep puddles here and there, and the hills ahead had vanished in a thick curtain of rain and mist.

Even Bron Melyn looked different as she turned the last bend and found herself facing it. The yard was empty and shining with water, the studio dark and shuttered. The tubs no longer had flowers in them; at some time during the week Alun must have replaced them with next year's bulbs, as he'd been talking of doing. He was already thinking of spring, but the general effect was dismal.

Slowly Linzi drove the Mini into the yard and stopped. She sat for a moment looking at the house, then got out. There was no point in waiting here. The rain lashed at her and she ran for the door, knocking on it hurriedly, and sheltering under the porch.

'Miss Berwick!'

Hugh had opened the door and was staring at her in astonishment. Suddenly at a loss, Linzi brushed back her russet hair, damp from the rain, and smiled at him.

'Hallo, Hugh. May—may I come in?'

'But of course! Miss Berwick—Linzi—we thought—yes, come in out of the rain. Have you driven here? Today? You must have had a terrible journey!'

'It wasn't the best,' Linzi admitted ruefully. 'Hugh, is Jason home?'

'Yes, he is.' Hugh's face was grave. 'I don't know how he'll take it, though—you coming back. He's been—well, not like himself at all these last few days.'

Linzi's heart sank. That didn't sound good. Briefly, she wondered if she'd done right to come. But she *had* to make that apology.

'Let me see him.' She smoothed her hair again and looked down at herself. She was wearing a rust-brown trouser suit that exactly matched the tawny shade of her hair and eyes, together with a white polo-necked sweater that effectively showed off her figure. 'Is he in the sitting-room?'

Squaring her shoulders with a boldness she didn't feel, she strode towards the sitting-room door and opened it.

Her heart was almost in her throat, beating against her ribs like a wild bird trying to escape from a cage, and her limbs trembled. She felt dampness in her palms and realised she was clenching her hands, the nails digging into the soft flesh. For a moment she held tightly to the handle of the door, gathering together all her courage. Then she took a deep breath and went in.

The room was almost dark. The heavy curtains were still drawn back to show the increasing gloom outside, the big window splashed with the rain that beat against it. In the fireplace was the comforting flicker of the log fire Linzi had imagined, the glow warming the old stone walls, reflecting from an old copper kettle that stood in the hearth.

Jason was sitting in his favourite armchair, close to the fire. A newspaper was spread across his knees, but he couldn't have been able to see the print for some time. He was quite motionless.

As Linzi came in, he said without turning his head: 'I think I'll take Bracken for a last run before it gets too dark, Hugh. He's getting lazy, stuck in front of this fire all day.'

Linzi swallowed. She wanted to say something and couldn't think of a thing. At last she opened her mouth, but before she could speak Jason had turned to see why Hugh made no answer. And she saw him rise, slowly, his jaw sagging, his face drained of all colour but the firelight, as he stared at her.

'*Linzi!*' he gasped. '*You*—what are you doing here?'

Linzi took a step forward. Her mouth was dry and her throat ached. She looked up at him with doubt in her eyes—was he pleased to see her or just plain shocked? 'I—I had to come,' she whispered. 'Jason, I——'

But Jason had already begun to recover himself. That first revealing response was already masked, and his face was stony again.

'You did?' he grated. 'And why, I wonder? To gloat— to revel in the sight of the proud Jason Carver, yearning for the one woman to refuse his favours? Well, look long and hard, Linzi Berwick, for this is the nearest you'll get to *that*!'

'*No!*' The negation was torn from her as she gazed piteously at him. 'Jason, I never meant—I didn't come for that. I wanted to——'

'To take up where you left off, perhaps,' he suggested sardonically. 'Make a fresh start, isn't that the phrase? And then you can do it all over again, can't you—lead me on and throw me down. In God's name, Linzi, why do you do it? Why do you get such pleasure from torturing me this way? What did I ever do to you, for heaven's sake?'

'Jason, it's not *like* that!' For the first time Linzi saw Jason clearly as a vulnerable human being, subject to the same emotions as she was herself, capable of being deeply hurt—capable of loving, even against his own will.

Making a tremendous effort to quell her trembling, she said: 'Jason, I've just driven down from London. I had to see you. You can turn me out afterwards if you like, tell me you never want to see me again, only please, *please* listen to me first. I can't go on without saying this to you.'

'You can't go on?' he said bitterly. '*You* can't go on? But *I* have to, don't I? Like I've had to these past five years—*I* have to go on.' He moved back to his chair and motioned Linzi wearily to the other. 'All right, let's get it over, whatever it is.'

Linzi sat down facing him. Her topaz eyes were huge in her pale face, and the chestnut hair fell softly to her shoulders, glowing in the light of the flames. She caught Jason's eyes fixed broodingly on her and saw with a pang how drawn and haggard he looked, the brilliant blue of his eyes dulled under the heavy brows, the silver dusting of his hair surely more noticeable than before. Surely all this could not have been brought about because of her? Had something else happened to bring that haunted look to his eyes?

'Jason, I saw Richard this morning,' she began hesitantly. 'He—he said he'd been here yesterday.'

'Oh yes, the banker.' Jason laughed harshly. 'He came

here looking for you. I had to tell him none of us had the faintest idea where you were, of course—he wasn't too pleased.'

'I was at my flat,' Linzi answered steadily. 'I'm sorry I didn't let you know. I didn't let anyone know—I wanted to be alone.'

'Second Greta Garbo, in fact,' Jason sneered. 'Well, go on with this fascinating tale. You saw Richard. When's the next thrilling episode?'

Linzi swallowed. 'Jason, you're not making this very easy for me.'

'Is there any reason why I should?' he countered swiftly.

'No. No, I suppose there isn't. It would just—help.'

Jason said nothing, and after a moment Linzi continued. 'Richard told me—he told me something very important. Important to me, anyway. He told me that Sian was here.'

Jason turned his head and looked at her. His face was inscrutable, but Linzi had the feeling that he had been expecting something different. 'So?' he asked, and his voice was cool.

'Jason, I was wrong about you and Sian—I know that now. You aren't her child's father, are you?' Now that she'd started, the words tumbled out. 'You never did seduce her—it was Selwyn, wasn't it? When he was here last year, before he went to America.'

'I don't really see why this should be important to you——' Jason began, but Linzi cut in.

'But it *is*! Because I thought—well, I thought that you'd been playing with her and then tried to dodge out of it. By implying that she'd been sleeping around anyway, and the baby could be anyone's. I thought it was a filthy thing to do,' she finished in a low tone.

Jason was staring at her, his brows drawn together, almost hiding the hard eyes underneath.

'Yes,' he said slowly, 'you're right. It *was* a filthy thing to do. But I didn't do it.'

'No, I know that now. And that's why I came—to apologise. I'm sorry I accused you of that, Jason. I'm sorry I ever thought it might be true.' Linzi's last words were spoken in a low, humble voice. She looked down at her hands; then looked up again to meet Jason's inimical glance.

'I'm sorry, too, Linzi,' he said, and his voice was harsh and grating. 'But the fact remains that you *did* think it. And no amount of apologising is going to alter that.'

'Jason, you knew I was thinking it, you could have told me the truth——'

'Yes, I could! But what difference would that have made? You *thought* it, Linzi—you thought I was *capable* of that kind of behaviour. My God!' He came to his feet and began to pace the room with a restlessness that betrayed the agitation inside him. 'You've known me all your life, we've lived as brother and sister, you ought to know me better than anyone else—and yet you could think *that* of me. What hope is there for any sort of relationship without trust?' He turned tormented eyes on her. 'It would have been better if you'd gone then. Better if you'd never come back. Now you've woken up all the feelings I'd thought had gone. You've started the torture all over again.'

Linzi gazed at him. *Jason* experiencing the reawakening of forgotten feelings? Jason, tortured by a love and longing that could never be fulfilled? With sudden hope, she half rose towards him—but his next words took her back to her chair, her heart sinking.

'I should have known there would be a snag,' he went on morosely. 'I've been telling myself all this week it's better to bring an end to it all now. I've just got to forget you and the—the feelings you rouse in me. And I thought I was succeeding—until you walked in the door a few minutes ago.' He turned a ravaged face to her. 'Linzi, what *are* you? Some kind of she-devil *Why can't you leave me alone?*'

'Why can't *I* leave *you* alone?' she gasped. 'Jason, *you* brought me here—*you've* kept track of me all these years!

I didn't even know where you were—I was making plans to marry Richard.' Overwhelmed, she buried her face in her hands. 'Why couldn't *you* have let things be? Now nothing's the same—I just don't know what's going to happen next. I don't know where to go, or what to do, and it's all your fault!'

'Oh, you've got nothing to worry about,' Jason retorted, his voice heavy with irony. 'You'll go back to your nice, safe banker and you'll live a nice, safe life, happy ever after. God knows what you'll do to each other, but it'll all be so dull you probably won't notice, so it won't matter anyway. And in fifteen, twenty years' time you'll be a comfortable matron, about three sizes larger than you are now, running the local whist drives and flower shows, going to school prize-givings to applaud your clever sons, entertaining your husband's business associates to smart little dinners, and you won't even remember all this. Except perhaps sometimes——' He suddenly strode over and gripped Linzi's arms, almost lifting her from her seat and letting his blazing eyes scorch her face as he spoke '—sometimes, when you'll look at some heather or some gorse, or maybe see a piece of sculpture, and then you'll think of the weeks you spent at Bron Melyn. I wonder if it will mean anything to you. Or will you just smile nostalgically and think what *fun* it all was?'

He finished with bitter sarcasm and threw her from him, so that she staggered and fell back into her chair. The tears streamed down her face as she gazed up at him. The picture he had painted was so horrifyingly real—so nearly the life she had seen for herself—and she wondered how she could ever have looked forward to such an existence. And then she realised that Jason didn't know—she hadn't told him that she'd broken off her engagement.

'But I won't be!' she cried. 'I won't be married to Richard—I broke it off this morning.' She got up and moved quickly towards him. 'I'm free, Jason—and none of that is going to happen!'

He made a quick, involuntary movement towards her, then withdrew. His eyes were hooded as he gave her a brief glance. Then he turned away, moving over towards the window.

'And do you really imagine that makes any difference?' he demanded harshly. 'My congratulations to Richard, of course—but surely you didn't come all this way just to tell me *that*!'

'No, I didn't.' Linzi's voice was dull and she turned back to the fire, suddenly icy cold. 'I came to apologise. I've done that—so now I'd better go.'

Jason nodded. 'You're driving back tonight?'

'I suppose so. Jason——'

'Take care, then,' he pursued, evidently determined to keep her at a distance.

'Yes, I will.' Linzi stood irresolute for a moment, then made up her mind. After all, she'd come knowing that this might be the result—but she still had nothing to lose if she made a final effort. And too much—everything—to lose if she didn't. She felt her love for Jason tingle through her body as she looked at him. He had his back to her again as he stared broodingly out of the window into the darkness; he looked huge, framed in the heavy curtains, but there was a set to his broad shoulders that she'd never seen before—almost a stoop, a sag of hopelessness. She had to try—for both their sakes, she had to try.

With a quick movement she was across the room, her arms around his waist, her head pressed against his back. She hugged him to her, her flesh warming to the contact, willing him to respond.

'Jason,' she said breathlessly, 'I can't leave like this. I love you, don't you understand? I think I always have. . . . You said the last time I was here that you wanted me and I wanted you, and you were right. Jason, I'm not asking for any promises. I'm not asking for anything—only one thing.' She pressed herself hard against him. 'Love me before I go, Jason—please! Love me just this once, so that we both have something to remember.'

Jason remained quite still. It was like hugging a rock. Then, slowly, he turned, and Linzi's blood leapt as he put his hands on her shoulders and looked gravely down into her eyes.

'You—you realise what you're saying?' His voice was a husky whisper and she could feel the thudding of his heart through the fabric of his sweater.

'I want you to love me,' Linzi answered steadily. She let her hands move against his back, sensuously outlining the firm muscles, the hard shoulder-blades. 'Jason, I've wanted you so much—I can't go away without—without——' Her voice broke as she gripped him to her, and she buried her face against his chest. Don't push me away now, she prayed, I couldn't bear it. Please, Jason, please. . . .

His sudden grip on her was convulsive as he gathered her against him, crushing her against his massive chest. Linzi felt one hand come up her back to spread its fingers in her hair, tangling it, lifting it away from her head as his lips sought hers blindly, dragging across her face from forehead to chin before finding her mouth. She let her own hands slide up towards his neck, caressing the nape, playing with his dark hair, and pressed his head closer to her own, her lips meeting and responding to his in a sudden rush of desperate longing. Her body moulded itself against his, the softness of her breasts crushed against him, the flatness of her stomach taut against his own. The hardness of his thighs moved against her and she gave a stifled gasp as fire spread through her body, tingling through her limbs and up her spine, weakening her legs so that she had to cling to him for support, and she knew by his muffled groan that the same flame had enveloped him too.

'Linzi!' he bit out, and with one movement he had swung her off her feet and was carrying her across the room to the couch which had been drawn up close to the fire. Gently he lowered her on to it, and she lay there looking up at him, her eyes dark in the fireglow, her tawny hair spread out on the soft, inviting cushions. Jason watched her in silence. He seemed to be struggling with himself and Linzi wanted to cry out to him, to beg him to waste no more time but to take her now, now before anything else could come between them. He was breathing quickly, his muscles tense against the tightened cloth of his jeans, and she reached up, letting her fingers trace a line up his thighs, watching as his face suddenly contorted with desire and he flung himself down beside her, his hands moving over her with an urgency that matched her own. With trembling fingers she felt for his waistband, sliding her palms up the warm skin under his sweater, feeling the roughness of the hairs against her soft hands. And felt his own hands, hard from the work he did, slip under her own sweater, pulling it over her head and fumbling for the catch of her bra so that he could pull it aside and expose the white perfection of her breasts, their nipples rosy and taut in the soft lambency of the firelight.

He caught his breath as he stared down at her; then with a swift movement he dragged his own sweater over his head, and snaked his body over hers. Gently, gently, he lowered himself against her so that the tightened nipples brushed against his hairy chest. He shifted himself down, then lowered his face to her breast and began to kiss her, encircling each breast with a ring of lingering kisses, letting his tongue tease the nipples into a stinging, throbbing ecstasy. Little fingers of fire began to radiate throughout Linzi's body, almost intolerable in their burning sweetness, and she stretched herself beneath him, her arms above her head, her face turning from side to side as she whimpered out her longing. Almost unable to bear his caresses any more, she reached down and dragged Jason's head up to her own, capturing his tormenting mouth and devouring his lips with hers.

'My love!' he muttered at last. 'Linzi, do you really

mean to tell me there's never been another man?'

'Never,' she whispered, taunting him with her eyes. 'There's never been another man I've wanted, Jason ... only you. ...' And she lifted her head to touch his lips with her own, sinking back as his mouth took triumphant command and his arms enfolded her once more closely against him.

'You realise there's no going back now?' he breathed moments later as his fingers found the zip of her trousers. 'It's too late to say no, Linzi. ... I've waited too long.' He slid the material down her thighs, slowly and sensuously, caressing the rounded curves as he did so. 'Whatever happens after this, you'll be mine—you realise that, don't you?'

'It's what I want,' she assured him, and arched her body in obvious invitation, a gesture he couldn't mistake. She heard his sharp intake of breath and her senses sang as he muttered something and drew away momentarily to wrench off his own clothes. And then, as he slid his body over hers and she reached up for him in final capitulation, they heard voices outside the room. Hugh's voice, and that of someone else. A woman. And as her horrified eyes met Jason's, Linzi knew with sickening certainty who it must be.

'Quick!' He thrust her clothes at her and reached for his own, dragging on jeans and sweater before returning to help her. Linzi remained on the sofa, too shaken to move, and ran quivering fingers through her dishevelled hair. She felt disheartended and angry. Was every opportunity of coming closer to Jason to be thwarted? Were they never to be able to enjoy their intimacy without being interrupted—and interrupted, moreover, by the one person in the world whom Linzi least wanted to see; Ceri, the girl Jason had been involved with, the girl who was determined to win him for herself.

They were scarcely composed, Jason in his chair and Linzi on the couch, each still breathing quickly and flushed with emotion, when Hugh knocked on the door. Dear Hugh, Linzi thought affectionately—at least he'd given them some time to recover themselves. She glanced at Jason with appreciation, and their eyes met as the door opened and Ceri came in.

The Welsh girl entered hurriedly, as if afraid that events were passing out of her control. Eyes flashing, she looked from one to the other, and Linzi knew that nothing was missed by that bright, sharp gaze. Involuntarily, she raised a hand to her tumbled hair and knew at once that it had been a mistake. Ceri's eyes were derisive and gleaming with spite as she watched the movement.

'So you're back!' she hissed, and Linzi saw Jason's eyes widen at the tone. 'I suppose you think you can just walk in and expect a welcome—take up right where you left off!' She whipped round to face Jason. 'I hope you've told her just where she gets off, Jason, because if you haven't I'll do it for you. It will be a real pleasure!'

'Jason hasn't——' Linzi began, but the venom in the other girl's voice silenced her.

'He *hasn't*? Perhaps he's too polite—too much of a gentleman. But *I* don't have to be so particular!' Ceri's red velvet skirt swirled as she swayed across the room to look down at Linzi, and her face was distorted with hate. 'You've been a thorn in my side ever since you arrived, Linzi Berwick, with your model figure and your smart American clothes. I told Jason he was making a mistake having you here, but you know what men are—he would have his own way. So what could I do? I just had to be patient—though I tried to warn you off a couple of times, only you were too stupid and too stubborn to see it!'

Linzi looked away from the hatred in her eyes. She saw Jason rise from his chair, looming over Ceri. But the Welsh girl had gone too far now to take notice of him; beside herself, she pointed a shaking finger at Linzi and ranted on.

'I thought we'd put paid to your games last week! When

Jason told me you'd gone and he didn't know why, I was sure we'd succeeded—*we* knew why, Selwyn and I, and we were pretty sure you wouldn't be coming back. And even more sure when your fiancé arrived last night. So what happened? Why *did* you come back? *What are you doing here now?*'

Helplessly, Linzi sought Jason's eyes. What was she to say? Should she descend to Ceri's level, enter into a slanging match, hurl at her the accusations which would make it quite clear just how Ceri had been planning her downfall? Something in Linzi's heart shrank from doing that—it would sully the love that she now believed existed between herself and Jason. She could not bring herself to fight over him with Ceri, like two dogs over a bone, could not bring into this room, still filled with the memories of their love, the sordid machinations that had so nearly driven them apart for ever.

She turned her head aside. Surely Jason wouldn't allow this to go on—wouldn't allow Ceri to harangue her in this way. Not so soon after he had held her in his arms and loved her?

'Jason,' she appealed, but the expression on his face baffled her.

'No, let Ceri go on. I'm finding this interesting.'

Ceri whipped round, her face triumphant. 'Thank you, Jason!' She turned back to Linzi. 'You see! He may not be able to resist you physically, but that's as far as it goes! Oh yes, I know—I saw you! You really ought to draw the curtains if you don't want everyone to know!' Linzi's eyes flew to the window, still unsheltered against the night, and her face flamed. 'Or perhaps you *did* want to be seen?' Ceri continued spitefully. 'Perhaps it's an added bonus—or perhaps you had some ideas of forcing Jason's hand? A shotgun wedding, perhaps, with witnesses. What a pity that your only witness should be me—and I'll never tell!' The pretty face was ugly now, and Linzi turned away, sickened. 'Yes, he's attracted to you all right—but then what man wouldn't be? That doesn't mean a thing! As I told you before, *I'm* the one he always comes back to—and that's the way it's going to stay.' She crossed the room and slipped her arm through Jason's, hugging it possessively. 'Isn't it, darling?'

Rigid now, Linzi watched as Jason looked down at the dark-haired girl, so tiny beside his bulk. He made no move to remove her; no shift in his stance took him any further from her side. But his face was expressionless as he let his eyes move slowly over the upturned face. She was willing him to kiss her, Linzi divined suddenly, and knew she was right as Ceri lifted herself on her toes, moving sensuously against him as she did so.

'Is it?' Jason said at last, reflectively. 'Well, you seem to know a lot more about this than I do, Ceri. Why don't you tell me more?'

Ceri's face changed. She pouted and shrugged her shoulders, pale against the dark red of her low-cut dress.

'Why, Jason, you're teasing me,' she exclaimed reproachfully. 'All right, so I spoilt your little bit of fun just now. But you're not going to hold that against me, are you?' She wriggled closer. 'After all, we can have plenty of fun ourselves, once *she's* gone.'

'Mm, I suppose we could,' he agreed thoughtfully. 'But I'm still waiting for you to tell me just why she should go. She *is* supposed to be working for me, after all!'

Linzi gasped. Just what was he playing at? Had he been stringing her along—taking what she'd so recklessly offered, an opportunist after all, intending that nothing should come of it? Was he still intent on revenge for what had happened five years ago? Tears stung her eyes as she watched him standing close to Ceri. The pretty, spoilt little Welsh girl was going to win after all—and now it seemed that there had never been any real doubt about it.

But Ceri, it seemed, was equally put out by Jason's ambiguous answer. She turned away, tossing her head a little, and flashed a glance of pure malice at Linzi. The firelight glinted on her dark curls and the ruby colour of her skirt glowed as she flounced away from Jason and flung herself into his armchair, slanting a provocative look up at him under her lashes.

'You're just being naughty now,' she grumbled. 'Teasing me. . . . Jason, why don't you just tell her to go?' she coaxed. 'We were so happy before she came along. We don't need anyone else, Jason. Just think how it used to be . . . you and me, alone here, the world shut out. . . . Don't you remember how it used to be?'

'Yes, I remember.' Jason paced to the window and drew the curtains across, closing out the storm which still lashed against the glass. 'But that's in the past now, Ceri. Like a lot of other things.' And as he turned and his eyes met Linzi's across the darkened room, her heart leapt.

Ceri was out of her chair in a flash, and this time all her barriers were down. Her breast heaved as she faced Jason, and Linzi guessed that this was the first time he had ever seen the real Ceri, malevolent and spiteful. Half frightened, she crouched back on the sofa.

'What do you mean?' Ceri breathed. 'In the past—me? *Us?* Jason, you don't know what you're saying! It's *not* in the past!'

'I'm afraid it is,' Jason answered calmly. 'I told you the other day—I've been telling you for weeks, months. What we had was fun, Ceri, I'm not denying it——' His eyes sought Linzi's again, almost in supplication. 'But that was all it was. You understood that as well as I did.'

'*No!* Never! I never intended——' Ceri broke off, her face flaming.

'You never meant it to stay on that level. You decided you wanted to marry me—because you needed my money to keep Penrhys Court.' Ceri gasped, but Jason went on inexorably. 'That was the real reason, wasn't it? The reason you did your best to prevent me inviting Linzi here. *The reason you told her lies to to get rid of her.*'

'*Lies?*'

'Yes, lies.' Jason crossed the room now and laid his hand on Linzi's shoulder. 'Oh, it isn't hard to guess where she got those ideas about me and little Sian. It still hurts that she believed them——' His fingers tightened momentarily and Linzi bowed her head. 'But how can I blame her? It's you who are to blame. You and that brother of yours.'

Ceri stared at them. Her fury seemed to twist her whole body, making it look ugly and deformed. Her eyes narrowed almost to slits, and her hands turned into claws as she lifted them. To Linzi's fascinated gaze she seemed almost to turn into a witch as she hissed at them.

'So you're taking *her*! *She's* won after all—or thinks she has. But do you know *everything* about her, Jason Carver? Do you know, for instance, what she was doing when she was in New York? The kind of pictures she was posing for there?' She turned a look of contemptuous anger on Linzi. 'Why not ask her? Or—better still—why not go and look in that rucksack you told me she'd left behind? I dare you, Jason Carver—*if you want to know just what sort of a girl Linzi Berwick is, go and look in her rucksack!*'

The silence was electric. Linzi stared at Ceri, and then, trembling in every inch of her body, turned her head slowly and looked up at Jason. His eyes were fixed on her, baffled and questioning. He glanced from her to Ceri and saw the look of triumph in the dark eyes. And as he turned back to her Linzi, with a gesture of despair, dropped her head into her hands.

'Linzi?' he said slowly, his voice rough and toneless. 'Linzi? What does she mean?'

But Linzi couldn't answer. There was no way she could explain, no way she could convince him. She could only beg, silently, that he wouldn't take up Ceri's challenge— that he wouldn't go to look.

But she might have known that that was hopeless. And when Jason left her side and strode heavily out of the room, she raised her face from her hands and looked bleakly at the older girl. She knew that at last the battle was over. It was impossible for her to stay any longer. She couldn't—she just *couldn't*—stay in the room while Jason pieced together those torn photographs, like some obscene jigsaw. She couldn't face the disappointment in his eyes— or the triumph in Ceri's.

'How did you know they were there?' she whispered.

Ceri's face was smug. 'Selwyn told me, of course. I was taking a chance that you hadn't thrown them out—but it was a chance worth taking. And it would have been easy enough to get replacements!' She paused, then said softly: 'You'd better go now. Before he comes back. It's the only way.'

'I don't know what you think you'll gain by this,' Linzi said shakily. 'Jason will never marry you now.'

'That remains to be seen. At least he'll never marry *you*.' Ceri lifted her pretty shoulders delicately. 'And he'll need some comfort, won't he?'

'You disgust me!'

'Do you know,' Ceri replied insolently, 'that doesn't worry me at all. Not one tiny bit.' She crossed to the door.' He'll be back soon. And I wouldn't like to be you when he comes.'

Defeated, Linzi walked to the door. She passed Ceri without a word; crossed the hall, praying that Hugh wouldn't appear; and let herself out through the front door into the wild darkness beyond. Half-blinded by tears, holding up her arms against the teeming rain, she blundered unseeingly across the yard to her car.

CHAPTER TEN

THE rain was now coming down almost too hard for the wipers to be effective. Uncaring, Linzi drove out of the yard and turned into the lane. She didn't know where she was going, hadn't even considered it. She wanted only to get away, away from Ceri's sneering triumph, away from the disillusionment in Jason's eyes when he saw the photographs. She should never have come at all, she told herself unhappily as she peered through the streaming windscreen. It had all been one terrible mistake, from start to finish. And the moments of rapture that she had experienced in Jason's arms made her loss all the more painful.

How could she have forgotten about the photographs? They were the very reason why she'd left Bron Melyn in the first place, yet since Richard had come that morning and told her about Sian she hadn't given them a thought. She might have known that the threat was still there; that as soon as Ceri and Selwyn discovered she was back the blackmail would be re-applied. But then she'd never really expected things to turn out as they had, she reminded herself. She'd thought that Jason would have remained bitter and angry, accepting her apology while not allowing it to make the slightest difference. As, indeed, he had done to begin with.

He had changed only when she had made her own positive approach to his physical desire for her. Knowing that he wanted her, she had made a deliberate assault on his senses, and it had worked as she'd known it must. And now even that would go against her. Jason would see the photographs, remember her apparently expert arousal of him—and draw the obvious conclusions. He would never again believe that she was still inexperienced, and all trust between them would be irrevocably destroyed.

Hopelessly, Linzi drove around the lanes, taking turnings without any real idea of where she was heading. In a very short time she realised that she was lost—but the knowledge ran off her mind as the rain was running off the car. What did it matter where she went? What did anything matter any more?

The dark hedges loomed above her as she twisted and turned through the winding lanes. What was Jason doing now? she wondered. Burning the evidence of her depravation, presumably; aided by Ceri, now soft and compliant again, ready to give the comfort she'd known he would need. And Ceri would accomplish that only too well, Linzi reflected bitterly. She was a born comforter, and with Linzi out of the way—for good this time—she would be making absolutely certain of her position in Jason's bruised affections.

Well, none of it would affect her any more. Somehow, it must be forgotten, put behind her. But that wasn't going to be so easy. It hadn't been easy five years ago, when she'd determinedly pushed away her schoolgirl crush and made a new life for herself. Then, she hadn't had any real idea of what she was giving up. Now she was only too well aware, and the knowledge was like a knife twisting in her heart.

Absorbed in her painful thoughts, Linzi only slowly became aware of the rough going of the car. Startled, she glanced out of the side window and realised that the hedges had vanished, and the relatively smooth surface of the tarmac lane had given way to uneven metalling. At some point, it dawned on her, she had come over the cattle grid and was now driving on the hill itself.

But which hill? She had no idea where she had been heading when she took her last turn; no idea which of the many lanes she had been in, or which track she was on now. Fighting a sudden panic, she felt the wheels of the Mini give a violent jolt, slip sideways and, as she clung to the steering-wheel, lurch into a deep pothole. The engine raced as the front wheels scrabbled at loose stones, but the car didn't move. It was firmly and irrevocably stuck.

Breathing hard, Linzi switched off the engine. The headlights still beamed ahead, cutting through what was now an eerie mist, but even as she watched the mist thickened and became dense fog which swirled around the car, probing the windows with long ghostly fingers and forming phantom shapes in front of her horrified eyes.

Reluctantly, she switched off the headlights, realising that it wouldn't help to run down the battery. The darkness was now impenetrable, with no glimmer of light anywhere, and Linzi fought down the rising hysteria of fear. There was nothing to be afraid of, she told herself unconvincingly. These were the mountains she loved, the hills that had welcomed her with such a glorious display of purple and gold. But their friendliness had vanished now; they were cold and hostile.

Well, she couldn't stay here all night. Already she was shivering, and although her luggage was still in the car she didn't fancy fumbling about to find warmer clothes. She couldn't be too far from the lane, anyway. All she had to do was walk back down the track and, sooner or later, she would come to a house.

Linzi reached forward to find the torch she always carried on the glove shelf. It was working, though not very bright, but ought to be enough to last until she reached civilisation. With a shivering glance at the swirling fog, she scrambled out of the car and locked it, wondering rather ruefully why she was bothering, since surely no one would be coming up here at this time and in these conditions. Then, turning her back on it, she set off along the track.

The track was rough, with boulders sticking up in it and loose rocks and stones among the running water and puddles that the heavy rain had caused. Linzi was thankful for her flat driving-shoes, but even so the going was difficult and she realised just how useful her boots would have been. Slipping and sliding, she made her way slowly along, picking out a way with the help of the torch. Now and then a startled sheep got up from the short turf and bounded away, startling Linzi even more. She slithered along, turning her ankle over more than once, and almost falling several times. She began to wonder if she had been wise to leave the car.

It seemed a very long way to the cattle grid. She supposed she must have crossed it several minutes before realising what had happened. But it was surprising that, even absorbed as she was, she hadn't noticed the extreme roughness of the track before reaching such a high point. It was even more surprising that the Mini had got so far. If she had seen the track in daylight she would never have dreamed of driving the little car along it.

She stumbled on, half crying. The rain and fog had soaked her through, her feet were sodden, and her hair hung lankly round her face, sending cold drips down her neck. The wind seemed to blow right through her, chilling her to the bone. And *still* she hadn't reached the cattle grid!

It was some time before Linzi admitted the truth at last. At some point she must have diverged from her track. Intent on picking out a way, she hadn't noticed any turnings; yet there must have been one—maybe more, she thought wretchedly—and she must have gone astray. Goodness knew where she was wandering now, but it wasn't going to lead her off the hill. The only thing to do was turn and get back to the car and start again.

It was over half an hour before she could bring herself to acknowledge the fact that she couldn't find the car.

Somehow she'd got herself hopelessly, entirely lost. If only she could find the car, she thought desperately, she could get back into it, stay there until morning and then find her way off the hill and get help. But unless she had an enormous stroke of good luck, it didn't seem likely that she was going to see her little Mini again. She was doomed to wander here—for ever, it seemed.

Linzi almost gave way to panic then. Still frightened by the loneliness, the eeriness of the fog and the sheer unfriendliness of the wild, empty mountains that surrounded her, she saw herself wandering here alone until, exhausted, she collapsed in the mud. She pictured herself falling, spraining an ankle or, worse still, breaking a leg and lying there helpless, unable to move, growing colder and colder. Who would find her? Who would even come to look for her? Jason would assume she had gone back to London. And even if he tried to telephone her, he would believe that once again she was simply not answering.

Linzi had completely lost hope now of ever finding her way. Recklessly, she plunged about, losing the track which had by then petered out into a narrow sheep-track through the heather. She found herself sliding down a steep slope, scrambling up again. She had no idea where she might be heading, knew only that she must keep moving. She even wondered why; but the instinct for survival kept her staggering on her feet.

The torchlight was growing dim now. Once or twice it flickered and she gave a sob of fear. She dared not let it run down altogether, and reluctantly she switched it off. Instantly, the darkness and fog closed in upon her, seeming almost to press physically down on her head, and she stood rooted to the spot, afraid to move.

After a few minutes her eyes grew accustomed to the darkness and she started forward again. She could just make out the dim shapes of rocks and sheep, though she couldn't tell which they were until they either got up and moved away, proving that they were sheep, or remained solidly where they were. She wondered if it might be possible to find a sheep that wouldn't move away, but would let her crouch against it. It didn't seem likely.

Very cautiously now, Linzi felt her way forward, all the time afraid that she would tumble into some hollow, even over a small cliff. The heather caught at her ankles and scratched them below the cord trousers, which were by now soaked and heavy as they flapped around her legs. More than once, she blundered into a gorse bush and had to extricate herself, painfully aware that some of the thorns remained in her hands.

She longed for Jason. With him, even the wild mountains and the sinister fog would be friends. He would know just which way to go, just where to find safety. Without him, she was lost and bewildered, and with a flash of insight she realised that this would apply all through her life; without Jason she would always blunder along, knowing neither where she was going nor how to get there.

Tears blended with the rain that streaked her face. Her meanderings were now completely aimless. Once or twice she wondered why she carried on, why she didn't just sink down in the heather and wait for whatever came. But she never did. Something drove her on; some faint glimmer of hope that she might somehow find another track, a track that would lead her to safety, to somewhere dry and warm.

But when her feet finally did find a track, she didn't believe it—didn't even realise it for the first few seconds, as she stumbled along its rocky way. Then it slowly dawned on her that she was no longer ploughing through heather and, hardly able to believe her good fortune, she switched on the torch.

It was a track, all right. A good, broad track, well used by the look of it. She had no idea which direction to take—it undulated along the contour of the hill, and she wasn't sure which way led upwards. But it was a track, that was the main thing, perhaps one of the old drovers' roads. Whichever way she went, it would surely take her somewhere.

Going very carefully, determined not to lose her way

again, Linzi picked her way along the path. It seemed to be leading her along a steep little valley; she could hear the rushing of a swollen stream below. Cautiously, she allowed herself to switch on the torch every few minutes to make sure that she hadn't strayed again. And after what seemed to be an interminable time, she found herself approaching something large, something that loomed ahead, black and sinister against the swirling fog, shining in the rain that poured down its sheer face.

Linzi stopped, half afraid. Was it a cliff—and would the track lead her safely over it, or did it go round in some way? She groped forward, then switched on the torch again, irrationally afraid of this huge obstacle. And then, as the dim light played over the grey stone, she gave a gasp of relief. It wasn't a cliff—it was a building! Derelict, for certain, but even so it might offer some kind of shelter.

She went forward and laid her hand against its bulk. It felt almost warm, friendly in this alien landscape. Keeping her hand against the wall, she crept round it.

But it didn't seem to be derelict. It was solid, without a crumbling stone in it. It led her round two corners without a break—and then she found the door—a good, solid door. And, to her infinite relief and joy, it moved under her touch, and she pushed it open.

Her heart hammering, Linzi stepped inside. For a moment, the relief of being out of the storm was enough. She leaned against the wall, revelling in dry air, in stillness accentuated by the raging of the wind outside, in comparative warmth.

But where was she? The place didn't appear to be occupied. No one had come to find out who was entering their house in the middle of the night. And who would be living up here anyway, so far from a road? Puzzled, Linzi switched on the torch again.

She seemed to be in a huge room. It was totally different from the small room she had expected, and she felt a leap of fear as the dim beam flickered up into the high roof. Then, as she looked around the walls, seeing the bookshelves, the armchairs and benches, the matting that covered the floor, it dawned on her at last where she was, and she gave a huge sigh of thankfulness, and her legs, so weary from their interminable stumbling through the heather, sagged so that she sank down on the matting and leaned her head against the wall.

She was in the chapel. The chapel Jason had taken her to that afternoon when they had walked together on the hills. The chapel where he had first begun to make love to her—where Ceri had interrupted them.

Linzi had no idea how long she rested there. But as the first intense weariness passed, she began to think again. She couldn't stay here on the floor, soaked and shivering, and now there was no need to. The chapel was well stocked with portable gas-lamps, and there was a gas cooker and two or three room heaters as well. There was probably even food, though she thought she was too exhausted to eat much. All she really wanted to do was get herself dry and warm and into that thickly-curtained bed at the other end of the chapel.

The torch lasted just long enough for her to find and light a lamp. By its steadier glow she was able to light one of the heaters, and then, grateful for its rapid warmth, she stripped off her soaked clothes, hanging them over chairs in the hope that they might dry a little by morning.

She couldn't find any towels, but the bed was covered with a ruby red candlewick bedspread. She wrapped herself in that and hugged herself dry in front of the heater. Then, totally worn out by her adventure, she crawled under the remaining bedclothes, sank thankfully into the soft warmth of the mattress, and fell fast asleep.

It was several hours later when Linzi woke. She had turned out the lamp when she got into bed, but the heater still gave off a comforting glow. She lay still, slowly remembering where she was and why. And now that the first shattering fatigue had gone, she felt again the sharp pain of loss. Tomorrow she would have to find her way back to her car, get help to get it back to the road, and then drive back to her lonely life in London. A sense of despair washed over her and, turning her face aside, she began to weep.

The tears were already soaking her pillow when she heard a sound. She was instantly alert. Was that what had woken her? She strained her ears and it came again— a sound of moving stones, a slithering noise, as if someone was blundering along the track outside just as she had done herself. And, as well as that, she could hear something else—a strange, animal snuffling.

A prickle of fear crawled along Linzi's spine. What could it be? Sheep didn't make that noise. Was it a pony? She'd seen them on the mountains, little Welsh ponies with delicate Arab faces and sturdy bodies. But a pony would make more noise than that, surely. And as she listened she heard a distinctly human voice. She sat up, her heart beating rapidly—and saw the door begin to open. . . .

'So *this* is where you are!' The voice was rough and male and overjoyingly familiar. Linzi flung herself from the bed and across the room. She wasn't even aware that she was completely naked. She just wanted to be in his arms, safe at last.

'Jason—oh, Jason!'

'Linzi!' She was enfolded in his embrace, held tightly against the wet sheepskin coat he was wearing. It was cold against her warm skin, but she didn't care. Sobbing with relief, she lifted her face and Jason immediately bent his mouth to hers.

'Linzi, thank God you're all right! I thought I'd never find you—I thought—oh, hell, I don't want to tell you what I thought!'

'I know.' She unbuttoned his coat and snuggled inside

it, pressing herself against his warmth. 'Jason, it was awful. I didn't know where I was, I——'

His hands moved over her body and she felt him realise her nakedness. With a muttered oath, he lifted her and carried her back to the bed, laying her in it with infinite gentleness. But Linzi would not allow him to move away. She kept her arms linked round his neck, holding him close. 'Come in with me, Jason,' she whispered, and heard his quick breath.

'Wait——' The word was torn from him as he gazed down at her with naked longing in his eyes. 'Bracken—he brought me here. I must dry him off——'

'Bracken!' Linzi sat up as Jason went over to the door. The great dog was lying just inside, his coat streaming with water, and she felt a pang of remorse that she hadn't even noticed him. She watched as Jason went to a cupboard and brought out an old towel that she hadn't found in her search. Then, as he began to rub the dog dry, she scrambled from the bed, wrapped a rug round her, and went to the stove.

'You must be cold too, Jason. I'll make us both a drink.' Love could wait a while, she told herself, and felt a warm security spread through her at the thought.

She made coffee with dried milk. The smell reminded her that she was hungry, and she foraged among the cupboards to see what provisions there were. By the time Jason had finished with Bracken, she had opened and mixed a tin of chicken soup with a can of beans and another of sausages. The resulting stew, served in bowls, with cracker biscuits from a packet, was unexpectedly appetising.

Jason came over to her side and watched as she ladled it out. Then he took her in his arms and nuzzled her hair.

'That looks marvellous,' he murmured, 'but isn't it a little too hot to eat straightaway?' And he bit gently at the lobes of her ears.

Linzi rested against him. The fire was already spreading

along her limbs, but this time the urgency had gone. She wanted to enjoy her longing, savour the delights as well as the pains of frustration. She was aware that up here in the chapel, with the storm raging even more fiercely than before, there was little chance of further interruption. They still had the whole night before them, and if they never had anything else it was going to be a night to remember for the rest of their lives. To hurry it would be a crime.

'Why don't you take off some of these wet clothes?' she murmured, letting her fingers stray up his chest, unbuttoning as they went. 'The bed's nice and warm . . . we can eat our supper there, and then——'

'Then?' he teased, capturing her hand in his and holding it to his lips.

'Then we can talk,' she said demurely. 'Unless you can think of anything else?'

'I just might, at that,' he muttered huskily. 'Linzi, you're doing it again . . . driving me wild . . . I don't know how much you think I can take. . . .'

'Not too much more, I hope,' she whispered, and felt his heart leap as she moved in closer and turned her face up for his kiss. 'But first, let's have this food. We're going to need our strength. . . .'

Jason uttered one muffled sound as he gripped her close against him, his hands seeking her softness under the rug she had wound round herself. Then she twisted away, picking up the bowls and carrying them over to the bed. She let the rug fall and slipped under the covers, then looked over at Jason and gasped involuntarily. He had slipped out of all his clothes and stood, magnificently naked, in the soft glow of the lamp, and she knew that it was as if the weeks between this moment and their first encounter here had never been. What had been started then was now about to be finished; it was as inevitable as the coming of morning.

Close together in the bed, they ate the stew and drank

the coffee. The warmth of the food spread itself through Linzi's body, comforting and relaxing her. When she had finished, she laid the bowl and the mug aside and turned to him, her body soft and yielding against him, her eyes large and dark in her glowing face.

'Jason,' she murmured softly, and slid her supple arms round him, drawing him close to her. She felt his hands on her shoulders, pressing her back on to the mattress, and then they moved down to cup her breasts as his eyes, almost black in the soft light, met hers and she knew that at last there were no secrets between them.

She put up her hands and let her fingers wander over his face, tracing the lines that had become etched there, recalling the contours that had always been so dear to her. Long nights in Paris, Rome and New York came back to her; nights spent alone but haunted by the memory of this face, the unbearable yearning to feel these arms around her. The finely-chiselled mouth was unsmiling, but its grimness had disappeared and its gravity came now from desire. Impulsively, she raised herself to kiss it; and with their lips pressed together, their mouths speaking in an older language than words, they fell back on to the mattress, each drawing comfort and reassurance from the intimate contact of their bodies; a comfort whose warmth was soon fanned into the white heat of desire.

A soaring joy swept through Linzi as Jason's body covered hers. She revelled in the length of it, the hardness of his thighs against hers, the massive breadth of his chest crushing her breasts. The rough hairiness of his body delighted her and she rubbed herself against him, closing her eyes in the joy of her own sensuality. Unable to get close enough, she arched her body towards his, and he gripped her close, his legs twining with hers, his hands exploring every inch and teasing her into little cries of passionate longing.

Sinuously, he lifted himself from her for the exquisite rapture of thrusting himself against her again. Linzi felt

an unexpected strength and energy flow through her limbs
as she responded eagerly to his caresses. Until now, she had
always imagined herself passive in this final joyous embrace;
instead, she was reacting with a fervour that astonished her
and brought a groan of pleasure from Jason's lips.

And then there was no more waiting, no more frustration. Linzi felt a stab of joy and then a pulsing ecstasy
that seemed likely to wrench her apart. Her body moved
of its own volition, and as she clung to Jason it seemed
that she was no longer in the bed, but somewhere else,
floating, flying, soaring in some bodiless world where
nothing else mattered, where only she and Jason existed,
fused in their love, and where nothing, nothing could ever
interfere with this incredible, exhilarating enchantment.

And then, when she thought she could bear no more, it
was over. Slowly, gently, she floated back to earth; back
to the high bed in the solid little chapel in the mountains.
Back to Jason's arms and the warm security of his love. A
contentment such as she had never known flooded softly
through her limbs, and she opened her eyes to stare be-
musedly up at his face.

'Oh, Linzi,' Jason murmured huskily. 'If that never
happens to me again, I won't complain, because it must
have been perfection. But—' his arms tightened around
her '—I hope, oh *God*, I hope it does happen again!'

'Jason, I love you,' Linzi whispered, half aware that
she had cried this out aloud only moments—or a life-
time—before.

'And I love you too.' His finger stroked her cheek and
his eyes grew sombre. 'Linzi, why did you do it? Run out
on me like that, yet again? Because of those pictures?'

She closed her eyes in sudden pain. 'I thought—I
thought you'd never want to see me again. They were
fakes, Jason—I didn't know they were going to use them
that way, the poses I did were perfectly innocent—but I
had no way of proving that. I didn't think you'd ever
believe it.'

'Oh, my darling!' He buried his face in her hair. 'Did you really think I'd believe that of you? Linzi, I've worked with you, I've seen you as a professional, I *know* you would never do that. Even if I hadn't loved you, I'd have known that.'

She let out a sigh. 'But Ceri—Selwyn——'

'I know all about Ceri and Selwyn and their nasty little game.' His face was grim again. 'After I found you'd gone I taxed Ceri with it and got the whole story out of her. My God, how she deceived me, the little witch! But I think she's got the message now. She won't be coming to Bron Melyn again.'

'Did—did she know they were fakes?'

'She did, though she wouldn't admit it. She knew she'd lost me, but she couldn't stand the thought that I might really love you.' His burning eyes searched her face. 'I don't know how to explain to you about Ceri. It was you all the time—all those years—but there were times when I thought you'd never come back, times when I was weak and craved some kind of love, even though I knew it was only second-class. I suppose I used Ceri in a way—but I knew she never really loved me, I knew that it was only self-gratification for her too, and I used that as my excuse.'

'Don't worry about it,' Linzi murmured, her hands moving slowly over his muscular back. 'It doesn't matter now—nothing matters now.' He lowered his lips to hers and, after a few minutes, she asked tentatively: 'What made you decide to use me as your model, Jason? Was it really because of the sculpture, or——'

He smiled at that. 'Yes, it was because of the sculpture—I knew as soon as I got the commission that here was my chance to do a figure I'd wanted to do for years— a figure symbolic of sun and freedom and grace, a figure that had been modelled on you in my head ever since I first conceived it. I *had* to have you for that—and it gave me my chance to bring you back into my life. I told you I kept tabs on you all those years, didn't I? I knew that the day would come when we'd have to come together again. I let you go five years ago—oh, because I was bitterly hurt, because I was angry too, but also because I did dimly understand why you went. And because I loved you, I let you go, to find your own way, to grow up. But I always intended that you should come back, though I didn't know how. And then two things happened. I got the commission—and I heard about your engagement.' He ran an urgent hand down her body and she shuddered with longing. 'I couldn't let things go any further, Linzi. I had to see you again—had to persuade you somehow that *I* was your man.' He grinned ruefully. 'I didn't make a very good job of it, did I?'

'Oh, you did,' Linzi assured him. 'I was in turmoil from the very first day. . . . But I'm glad you did it, Jason.'

'Are you?' His lips took hers again and his hands moved more tensely over her skin. 'And now? You *will* marry me this time, won't you, Linzi, my sweet? No more running out on me? You promise?'

'I promise,' she said steadily, but he still wasn't satisfied.

'I think I'll lock you up until our wedding day,' he muttered. 'Lock you up and set Bracken to guard you. . . . Do you know, he brought me here to you tonight? I tried to follow you through all those lanes, and I'd almost given up hope when I noticed fresh tracks in the mud and realised you'd gone up into the hills. And when we found your car—I nearly went mad, Linzi, imagining all kinds of things. But Bracken never wavered. He took me up and down paths, through the heather, sometimes going in circles, sometimes apparently going nowhere, but he never gave up. And in the end he brought me here.'

'Dear Bracken,' Linzi said softly. 'We'll take him on our honeymoon with us.'

'Honeymoon?' Jason exclaimed in mock horror. '*Honeymoon?* And what makes you think we're going on honeymoon? We've got *work* to do, woman—I've *still* got that figure to finish!' He drew her to him again and enfolded her in his arms. 'We'll go away after that, I promise you, wherever you like. But I can tell you this, Linzi, my dear, sweet love—our life is going to be one long honeymoon. And after waiting five years, I don't think that will be any more than we deserve!'

And as she welcomed his love again, Linzi saw the first grey spears of dawn creep into the high, narrow windows, and she knew that what he said was true. And all the cares and unhappiness of the past five years were shed as they made love with a sweet, rapturous abandon that transcended anything that had gone before.

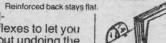

4 FREE
Harlequin Romances